Lliswerry High School
Newport, Gwent

BEETHOVEN'S
STRING QUARTETS

Beethoven's
String Quartets

PHILIP RADCLIFFE
Fellow of King's College, Cambridge

CAMBRIDGE UNIVERSITY PRESS

Cambridge

London   New York   Melbourne

Published by the Syndics of the Cambridge University Press
The Pitt Building, Trumpington Street, Cambridge CB2 1RP
Bentley House, 200 Euston Road, London NW1 2DB
32 East 57th Street, New York, NY 10022, USA
296 Beaconsfield Parade, Middle Park, Melbourne 3206, Australia

First published 1965 by Hutchinson University Library, London
Second edition 1978

First printed in Great Britain
by The Anchor Press, Ltd
Reprinted in Great Britain
at the University Press, Cambridge

Library of Congress Cataloguing in Publication Data
Radcliffe, Philip
Beethoven's string quartets
Includes index
1. Beethoven, Ludwig van, 1770–1827. Quartets, strings
I. Title
MT145.B425R3   1978   785.7′4′71   77–26271

ISBN 0 521 21963 9   hard covers
ISBN 0 521 29326 X   paperback

To

WINTON DEAN

Contents

Preface

The enormous extent of the existing Beethoven literature is not, on the face of it, encouraging to the writer of today. But it can also be seen as a testimony to the endless fascination of his music. The string quartets have never been as much in the public eye as the orchestral works, but their appeal has deepened steadily and it is hard to imagine it ever diminishing. This book aims at giving a comprehensive view of them, not as an isolated phenomenon but in relation to the rest of Beethoven's output, stressing at the same time the variety and consistency of Beethoven's development. It has been written in the hope that the last word has not yet been said on this boundlessly interesting subject.

P.F.R.

1

Introductory

LIKE the work of many great artists, Beethoven's music has produced very different reactions at different times. For many years the approach to it was dominated by the picture of a tragic rebel, perpetually shaking his fist at destiny; great emphasis was laid on the works of his middle period, especially those associated with some kind of extra-musical programme or message, the early works being patronised as immature and the latest dismissed as incomprehensible. A reaction against this attitude led to a tendency to regard him as a much over-rated composer who, towards the end of his life, somehow contrived to write some fine string quartets. The division of his creative life into three periods is helpful up to a point, but it has sometimes led people to refer to early, middle and late Beethoven as though they were practically three different composers. It is perhaps easier now for us to see how Beethoven's style could at the same time develop im-measurably and yet continue to be the expression of a highly independent personality.

The quartets give as full and varied a picture of this person-ality as do the symphonies and the sonatas; their whole character is, however, inevitably affected by the medium for which they were written. In his earlier years it was the piano that stimulated Beethoven to his boldest flights of imagina-tion, and in the early quartets there is nothing as passionate as the slow movements of some of the sonatas of that period, such as Op 10, No 3, in D major. The Op 59 and Op 74 quartets are rich and massive in texture, but do not show the stormy explosiveness of the 'Appassionata' Sonata, or the first movement of the fifth symphony. It is not surprising that, in his last years, his increasing interest in polyphony found particularly full expression in the writing of string quartets. Chamber music for strings alone is one of the most subtle and sensitive forms of composition: for it to be completely successful it is essential that the medium should seem to have been chosen by the composer for its own sake and not as a makeshift for something else. The distinction of having been the first composer to write a string quartet has been claimed by various writers for various musicians, including Allegri and Alessandro Scarlatti; but these cannot be regarded as more than flashes in the pan, and it was not until halfway through the eighteenth century that the quartet became firmly established. In the seventeenth century, however, many works for viols were written in England, and it is worth for a moment comparing the growth of this kind of music with that of the string quartet in the latter half of the eighteenth century.

The fantasy for viols began as an attempt to transfer to instruments the kind of polyphony that had already been used extensively for choral music. But it soon became apparent that instrumental works of this kind needed a less predominantly contrapuntal texture and more clearly defined and vividly contrasted thematic material; also the increase of instrumental technique led to a more percussive and incisively rhythmic style. Similarly in the eighteenth century, chamber music, especially for strings alone, could not become a major branch of composition until it could stand on its own feet, independently of orchestral music; and this could not happen until composers ceased to depend on the harmonic support provided by the continuo. This was a very gradual process: at the time when Haydn was forming his style, the distinction between orchestral and chamber music was still imperfectly realised. One of his earliest quartets exists also as a symphony, and occasionally, even in much later works, he still seems unconsciously to be thinking in terms of the orchestra and to forget that the cello is not being doubled by the bass an octave lower. Composers could still afford to use a comparatively slight and sketchy texture, especially in the simpler and more lyrical movements, whether in a symphony or in a quartet. But it is fascinating to trace the steady increase of sensitiveness in Haydn's music. In the symphonies the treatment of the orchestra becomes more and more varied and subtle, culminating in the wonderfully imaginative scoring of the last works; and in the quartets the texture, very simple in the early ones, becomes increasingly flexible, largely as a result of Haydn's wonderfully fresh and spontaneous counterpoint.

It is worth dwelling for a while on these works, for of all Beethoven's predecessors Haydn is the one to whom he was most indebted. Neither composer could quite equal Mozart in fluency of melodic invention; both were intensely interested in thematic treatment and possessed an imagination that enabled them to see possibilities in seemingly insignificant ideas. It was hard for any composer of that period not to be affected by Italian opera, and its influence on Mozart was, of course, very deep; his sensitiveness to detail enabled him to turn the florid language of coloratura into something wholly personal and intimate. Neither Haydn nor Beethoven absorbed it to the same extent, though it played a more important part in Beethoven's music than has often been suggested. But Haydn's most characteristic tunes are broad and simple; they occur less frequently in his piano music, as he had little faith in the sustaining power of the keyboard instruments of his day, but they are often to be found in his other instrumental works and especially in the quartets. In the slow movements of the quartets in D major, Op 76, No 5, and G major, Op 77, No 1, there is a solemnity of a kind that is usually associated with Beethoven but can frequently be found in the later works of Haydn; a fine instance is the Largo from the Symphony No 88 in G major, which must have made a special appeal to Beethoven, as there are five reminiscences of it in his music, in works extending from Op 10 to Op 110. Now and again in Haydn's later works can be found the influence of Mozart's subtle and sensitive chromaticism, but in general the harmonic highlights in his music are at the same time bolder and simpler; a fine instance occurs early in the slow movement in the Quartet in G minor, Op 74, No 3. Effects of this kind undoubtedly left their mark on Beethoven and also on Schubert. But a still stronger bond between Haydn and Beethoven is their humour, which is decidedly different from the urbane gaiety of Mozart; it is more forthright and abrupt, often involving unexpected turns of phrase that must have seemed very disconcerting to their more conventional contemporaries. In both composers a jocular manner can sometimes be combined with an odd sense of dramatic suspense and uncertainty. Haydn was a less explosive personality than Beethoven and disapproved of his more aggressive outbursts, whether serious or comic; but fundamentally there was much in common between the two composers, and though they did not get on particularly well, Beethoven always felt a deep respect for Haydn.

The string quartets of both composers represented a very important part of their output: those of Mozart, despite the supreme beauty of the greatest of them, are more uneven as a whole and do not give so continuous an idea of the development of his style. The first twelve are early works of no great individuality, the last six showing strongly the influence of Haydn's Op 20, and there was a gap of some ten years before the magnificent set of six dedicated to Haydn. These are his greatest quartets and the mysterious chromatic introduction to the sixth may well have influenced that of Beethoven's third 'Rasumovsky' Quartet; the remaining four contain much delightful music, but do not rise to the heights of the string quintets that he wrote during his last years. It would hardly have been possible for Beethoven in his earlier works to have escaped the influence of Mozart, but it is less notable in the quartets than in some of the other chamber works, especially those for wind instruments. Inevitably, in the early works of Beethoven there are innumerable turns of phrase that can be found not only in Mozart but in the work of any composer of the period. There are several works, including one of the quartets, that show signs of being modelled closely on a work by Mozart; these occasions always show Beethoven's independence, though not necessarily his superiority. There are certain moods in Mozart that have a foretaste of Beethoven: the defiance of C minor and the more sombre and foreboding atmosphere of D minor; sometimes also a kind of spaciousness, as in the first movement of his String Quintet in C major. Beethoven could frequently achieve a polished and unobtrusive profundity of the kind generally associated with Mozart, but this could not be fully realised until his idiom had become thoroughly individual, in the gentler and more lyrical works of his second period, which are fully as characteristic and significant as those of stormier vein. The texture of Mozart's quartets is always a delight to the ear, but that of Haydn's is more varied, ranging from the almost orchestral richness of some of the later slow movements to the bleak canonic writing of the Minuet from the D minor Quartet, Op 76, No 2, and the extraordinarily sonorous two-part opening of the Andante from Op 77, No 2. His phrase-lengths are also more varied on the whole, especially in the later minuets, which in their wayward imaginativeness come very near the mood of some of Beethoven's scherzos. Both Mozart and Beethoven would have been the last to deny their debt to

Haydn, especially in the writing of string quartets. For Mozart, with his innate feeling for musical beauty of all kinds, the forms and manners of his time were, in the words of George Dyson, 'the most innocent and engaging companions', which could, if required, be modified in detail, but were not in need of any drastic alteration or enlargement. Haydn and Beethoven had less fluency and ease, and, perhaps for that reason, were more venturesome and intellectually curious in their approach to composition.

During the latter half of the eighteenth century there were other composers of string quartets, but it is very doubtful whether any of them would have had much effect on Beethoven's style. Haydn's pupil Ignaz Pleyel wrote a large number, which spoke in the current idiom of the day fluently and amiably, but with no individuality. More prolific still was Boccherini, who always wrote admirably for the instruments, in a spacious and flowing style. But his most important work is to be found in his string quintets, which give more scope for the picturesque instrumentation that was probably his greatest gift. His quartets are pleasant, but in harmonic or rhythmic variety and vividly memorable invention they fall far short of Haydn. Dittersdorf, though primarily a composer of comic opera, wrote six quartets which are unpretentious but have an attractively wayward character that might well have appealed to Beethoven. If the themes of Boccherini reflect the ornate and leisurely flow of Italian *opera seria*, those of Dittersdorf speak in the crisper and more concise language of the German *Singspiel*. His modulations are bold and unusual for the period, and often lead to delightfully unexpected digressions; sometimes there are original points of construction, such as the return of a few bars of the Alternativo at the end of the Quartet in C major.

Of all the pre-Beethoven composers of string quartets Haydn undoubtedly covered the widest range; the legend of the eternally playful and good-humoured 'Papa Haydn' has by now been thoroughly discredited. In his later work there can often be found a wealth of deeply felt emotion, sometimes serene, sometimes tragic, and his whole approach to composition was extremely enterprising and versatile. In many ways Beethoven's earlier works are a kind of extension and intensification of those of Haydn; sometimes more vehement and sometimes more serene; sometimes more expansive and sometimes more concentrated. The contrasts are more vivid and the manner, especially in the piano works, often more explosive. In the shorter movements the different ideas succeed each other more abruptly and when the music is on a larger scale the harmonies move with greater deliberation. This results in a spaciousness which is one of the most distinguishing features of Beethoven's style, sometimes giving a feeling of deep serenity and sometimes of prolonged suspense. Among the earlier works it is felt most notably in the piano sonatas, often in passages that suggest an inspired improvisation; it appears from time to time in the Op 18 quartets and still more in Op 59. Mention has already been made of the spaciousness of the first movement of Mozart's String Quintet in C major; that of Beethoven's first 'Rasumovsky' Quartet begins in a rather similar way, with the same mixture of repeated chords and slowly moving harmonies, but it is considerably more leisurely, with passages which could only make their effect in a movement planned on a very large scale. But spaciousness of this kind does not, in Beethoven's finest work, depend entirely on size; in his last period he could achieve it in highly concentrated movements like the opening Allegretto of the A major Piano Sonata, Op 101, or the Allegro molto vivace from the String Quartet in C♯ minor, simply by broadening the harmonic movement. It is not surprising, however, that he could not do this thoroughly until he had written enormous works such as the third symphony and the first 'Rasumovsky' Quartet.

One of the most striking features of Haydn's later work is his love for remote keys, sometimes for central movements or sections of movements and occasionally for modulation inside a movement; particularly impressive are the trios of some of the later minuets, which are often in a key a third above or below the tonic. Effects of this kind play an increasingly important part in Beethoven's music; when they occur during the course of a movement it is not done in quite the unconcerned lyrical manner of Schubert, who will often modulate to unexpected keys while a theme is in progress, but usually with a kind of awe-inspiring simplicity and directness. The transition from the second to the third variation in the slow movement of the Quartet in E♭ major, Op 127, is a wonderful and very characteristic instance, though to Haydn, had he lived long enough to hear it, and indeed to many other younger musicians, its simplicity might have seemed merely crude. Beethoven's attitude to opera was highly critical, but it has already been suggested that he owed a certain amount to its idiom. The most widely familiar tunes by Beethoven are admittedly of a simple nature, moving mainly by steps, but all through his life he quite often used a more florid and luxuriant melodic idiom. For this, Mozart, with his uniquely beautiful blend of Italian melodic fluency and German harmonic sensitiveness, was inevitably a powerful influence. In the slow movement of the String Quartet in G major, Op 18, No 2, for instance, the decorative melodic writing has a decidedly Mozartian character; in the Adagio of the Piano Sonata in G major, Op 31, No 1, composed about a year later, there are passages of a similar kind, but here they seem slightly archaic owing to the more advanced harmonic character of the movement as a whole. In Beethoven's later works, though he never lost his love for long, florid sweeps of melody, they become more essentially instrumental in character and proportionately less like Mozart, whose melody almost always had decidedly vocal inflections. The viola melody of the second variation in the Finale of Beethoven's Quartet in E♭ major, Op 74, is simply a decoration of the theme against a very simple harmonic background, such as Mozart frequently wrote. But it could not be by Mozart; the line is less smooth and the chromaticisms stand out in stronger relief. When passages of this kind occur in the late piano sonatas they are of an essentially keyboard character, and sometimes have a strong foretaste of Chopin; the transitional theme in the Adagio of Op 106 and the first variation of the Finale of Op 109 are marvellously beautiful instances. The slow movements of the ninth symphony and the quartet, Op 127, contain passages of a similarly ornate character which are equally suited to the violin in their widely sweeping melodic curves. Beethoven, like so many of the greatest composers, could absorb influences of various kinds, turning them into something entirely individual. His natural approach to music was instrumental rather than vocal and he is reported to have said that whenever an idea came to him he always heard it on an instrument; at the same time he was able to learn much from certain kinds of vocal music without being overwhelmed by them.

His creative life was considerably shorter than that of Haydn, but it cannot be denied that in it he covered a wider range. Yet, though he travelled a long way from the style of his early works, he was a less conscious innovator than several later composers, including Wagner, and the differences of character between his earliest and latest works are on the whole less fundamental than those between *Rienzi* and *Parsifal*. His treatment of traditional forms was infinitely varied and considerably more flexible than that of many later composers, but he did not need to abandon them completely. In his last works the texture became increasingly contrapuntal, but if occasion demanded he did not scorn to use a simple and stereotyped accompaniment figure. In works of the third period it is not uncommon to find individual phrases that could easily have appeared in much earlier works, and even in the last quartets some of the lighter themes have a decidedly Haydnesque character. In these works it is not the language itself that is new but the manner in which the words are used. Sounds that are familiar in themselves appear in unusual sequences, often with the emphases in unexpected places; cadences come less frequently, and sometimes so casually as to be hardly noticeable. Points are liable to be made with an almost telegraphic terseness and the texture is often exceedingly sparse. For many years this was a severe stumbling-block, especially to audiences accustomed to the full rich sound of Op 59 and Op 74. Even as late as 1911, T. F. Dunhill, in his book on chamber music, expressed the view that the late quartets were imperfectly realised sketches, in which Beethoven's inner ear had been obscured by his deafness. For a long time a halo of mystery surrounded these works, and performances were decidedly rare. During the 1890's, however, Bernard Shaw hailed with delight a performance of the C♯ minor Quartet, and when reviewing it referred to the 'simple, straightforward, unpretentious, perfectly intelligible posthumous quartets'; it would be interesting to know whether he knew the 'Grosse Fuge'. During the present century these quartets have often been praised for the very reasons for which they were previously criticised; their frequent abruptness and spareness made a strong appeal to those who had reacted against the more spacious style of the middle period works. But in works of so individual a character it is easy, and also misleading, to stress certain aspects at the expense of others.

Beethoven, like Bach, had many facets to his musical personality, and this is true not only of his last works but of his whole output. His first period has been described as the period of imitation, but this does not take into account the

independence and imaginativeness of its beṣt works. Similarly
the second period is usually associated with the familiar large-
scale works, heroic and spacious in manner, but it has already
been suggested that their more intimate and lyrical contemporaries, such as the fourth piano concerto, the Piano Sonata
in F♯ major, Op 78, the Violin Sonata in G major, Op 96, and
many others show an entirely different but equally important
aspect of Beethoven's personality. In the works of the last
period there is an element of bareness and austerity which,
partly owing to the nature of their medium, finds particularly
full expression in the posthumous quartets. But those who, on
the strength of this, exalt these quartets at the expense of all
Beethoven's other works show a very incomplete understand-
ing of his music. The style of his third period can show the
most monumental spaciousness in such works as the ninth
symphony, the Mass in D and the Piano Sonata in B♭ major,
Op 106, and the richest and mellowest lyricism in the sonatas
Op 109 and 110; and, to return for a moment to the quartets,
it is worth remembering that Op 135, which is perhaps the
tersest and sparest of them all, also contains a slow movement
which, in its simple and darkly coloured solemnity, shows
kinship with the Andante of the 'Appassionata' Sonata. Since
Beethoven's death his music has been appreciated, sometimes
for this quality and sometimes for that; perhaps, at long last,
it has now become possible for us to get a clearer and more
comprehensive view of it all.

2

Op 18

BY 1801, the year in which the Op 18 quartets were published, Beethoven had already composed a considerable amount of chamber music, which falls into various categories. The works that include wind instruments are on the whole the most conventional, though they are extremely effective in performance and the Serenade in D major for flute, violin and viola has very great charm. The works for piano and strings have more individuality; the two sonatas for cello and piano, Op 5, are full of ideas, though rather diffuse, and the three trios for piano and strings, Op 1, include the very fine and striking work in C minor. It is surprising that, before attempting a string quartet, he should have written several works for the far more difficult medium of the string trio. The first of these, in E♭ major, Op 3, is obviously modelled on Mozart's magnificent Divertimento in the same key; it inevitably falls short of this, though there are signs of individuality. The Serenade in D major, Op 8, is a light-hearted work that refuses to be overawed by its medium, sometimes treating it almost as though it were a brass band. But the three trios, Op 9, are of greater importance, and contain some of the best music that he had yet written. The Finale of the first trio, in G major, looks ahead to Beethoven's later *moto perpetuo* finales; it is interesting that its theme appears to have been first sketched in the augmented form that eventually was not introduced till near the end of the movement. The Trio in C minor opens with a theme that seems to have haunted

Beethoven years later, when he was writing the tremendous Finale of the C♯ minor String Quartet. In all these works the sonority of texture is remarkable and is achieved without any feeling of strain.

Of the Op 18 quartets, the first in order of composition is the work in D major that was eventually published as No 3. It has never been one of the most popular, and contains nothing as deeply emotional as the Adagio of the Quartet in F major, nor has it the sparkle of No 2, in G major, or the prophetic quality of the 'Malinconia' section of No 6. But it is full of beauty of a quiet and thoughtful kind, which becomes more apparent the better the work is known. The unceremonious opening, with the first violin unsupported, looks back to Haydn's Op 50, No 6 in the same key, and the quiet sustained harmonic background suggests the first movement of Haydn's 'Sunrise' Quartet in B♭ major, from Op 76. But in both of the Haydn movements the leisurely openings soon give place to more energetic music; in Beethoven's there are two big climaxes, but the general atmosphere is more contemplative. The conventional contrasts of mood between first and second subjects are a good deal less common in Beethoven's music than is sometimes imagined. Even in the first movements of the fifth symphony and the 'Appassionata' Sonata, he does not allow the lyrical second theme to luxuriate as many later composers would have done. Continuity of structure was always of the utmost importance and in the Finale of the Piano Sonata in C♯ minor and the first movement of the 'Pastoral' Sonata, both written in 1801, he is concerned with maintaining a single mood throughout a movement in sonata form, stormy in the one and idyllic in the other. In the first movement of the D major Quartet the atmosphere is somewhat more varied, but it has an admirable continuity; the spontaneous ease with which the transitional theme grows out of the two semibreves from the first subject is particularly happy. There are many delightful features in this movement: the unexpected modulation at the beginning of the second subject, the beautifully contrived return of the main theme after the development, which foreshadows some of Mendelssohn's most imaginative passages, and the short but eventful coda, with its very effective reminiscence of the second subject in a remote key.

The Andante con moto in B♭ major is based on a very simple theme which, in the hands of an inferior composer, could easily have seemed pedestrian and commonplace, but is here treated with great sensitiveness. There are some episodic passages of great delicacy, but for the most part the texture is very rich; the harmony is often more luxuriantly chromatic than that of Haydn or Mozart, but is saved from being oppressive by the constant interest of the individual parts. The movement is in rondo form, the central episode being devoted to development of the main theme; it is treated with much resource, its appearance in the bass in D♭ major having the dark solemnity that is usually associated in Beethoven's mind with that key. The coda is also remarkable; animated passages in triplets alternate with new and mysterious developments of the theme and the last twelve bars are exquisitely coloured. This may not be one of the most expansive or immediately appealing of Beethoven's slow movements, but it becomes increasingly attractive with further acquaintance, and its thoughtful and subtle character is well suited to the general atmosphere of the whole quartet.

The third movement, like a fair number of others in Beethoven's works, is not described as either minuet or scherzo, but is simply marked 'Allegro'. Despite its quiet and unassuming manner, it is a very interesting and individual piece of music. At the time when it was written, any well brought up composer, when writing in a major key, would almost invariably make his first modulation go to the dominant. Beethoven, however, makes his first section end in the mediant minor, a modulation very common later in the nineteenth century, but very unusual at so early a stage in the movement in 1800. Having done this, he passes through several other keys, but still avoids the dominant; the opening phrase, though frequently referred to, does not return in its original form. The final cadence is postponed for some time and eventually arrives in an unusual way, after some attractive passing dissonances, the effect of which is lost if the movement is played too fast. There is a short trio in the minor, after which, instead of the usual *da capo* sign, the main part of the movement is written out again with some amplification of colour. The more obviously great qualities of Beethoven's music have tended to blind people to his capacity for the flowing, comparatively relaxed lyrical mood of which this movement is a characteristic and delightful specimen. The Finale of the Quartet in D major is more markedly Haydnesque in manner than the rest of the work; the first movement of the 'Clock' and the last of the 'Military' Symphony have obviously influenced it. In both of these, however, the springing energy is now and again tempered by moments of almost uncanny stillness. Beethoven at this stage could not quite achieve this, though there is a suggestion of it at the end of the development. The high spirits of the movement are unflagging, sometimes with a touch of ferocity, and the passages of suspense when the first three notes of the theme are tossed from one instrument to another look ahead to the second 'Rasumovsky' Quartet. One of Beethoven's favourite ways of ending a movement is with a *diminuendo* that gradually sinks to *pianissimo* and is then shattered by a sudden *fortissimo*. Here we have the reverse process: a big climax is followed by rapid collapse and a quiet reminiscence of the first three notes. The slightly earlier Piano Sonata in G major, Op 14, No 2, ends in a rather similar manner; in the quartet the effect is more comic, owing to the preceding climax. In both cases the unceremonious end is particularly suited to the intimate and informal character of the works and is of a kind that is a good deal commoner in Beethoven's sonatas and chamber music than in his orchestral works.

The Quartet in F major, published eventually as No 1, is a larger work and more varied in mood. The opening of the first movement, which seems so spontaneous, cost Beethoven an infinite amount of trouble and it is interesting to trace the stages by which it came into existence. The original sketch:

Ex 1

in common time, bears no relation whatever to the final version except for the first five notes, and even they are in a different rhythm. It soon became clear, however, that these opening notes were to be the operative feature of the theme. Eight more versions followed, all in common time; finally, in the ninth, the familiar triple time appears:

Ex 2

It is amusing to see how Beethoven, having at long last found the rhythm that he wants, is so pleased with it that he cannot keep away from it for long. The atmosphere of the movement is very different from that of the flowing and thoughtful Allegro of the D major Quartet; the rhythmic element is far more predominant. Even in the lyrical second subject, which is not allowed to play more than a subsidiary part, the most notable feature is an unusual and attractive grouping of notes. But all through the exposition the first theme is the dominating factor; it guides the delightful transition passage and frequently reappears in later stages, the rhythm sometimes remaining, like the grin of the Cheshire cat, without the melodic line. In the development its treatment is admirably varied; first in increasingly close contrapuntal imitation and then, when this has reached its climax, in a very simple texture with repeated chords and slowly moving harmony; this is a particularly characteristic moment. There are fresh adventures in the recapitulation, and at the beginning of the coda a feeling of suspense is produced by the introduction of an entirely new theme, which is worked contrapuntally with the first. The brittle texture and half-jocular manner of the movement look back to Haydn, but the tension is more acute and the gestures more abrupt.

The most striking part of the Quartet in F is undoubtedly the second movement, headed 'Adagio affettuoso ed appassionato'. The word 'affettuoso' was used quite frequently in the earlier part of the eighteenth century and 'appassionato' in the nineteenth, but both were unusual in 1800. The movement is said to have been inspired by *Romeo and Juliet*; whether or not this is true, the unusually elaborate directions suggest that Beethoven felt himself to be writing a specially emotional piece of music. Haydn and Mozart wrote surprisingly few slow movements in minor keys, especially in their later works; those by Beethoven are more numerous and almost all of exceptional quality, the earliest outstanding instance being the very sombre and passionate Largo e mesto from the D major Piano Sonata, Op 10, No 3. The Adagio of this F major Quartet has something of the same passion, but it is considerably more restrained and the rather unusual 9/8 tempo gives it a more luxuriant melodic flow. It is a fine specimen of Beethoven's early style in its more Italianate vein, with suggestions of Mozart, but with bolder outlines and stronger emphases. It is in full sonata form. In contrast to the long opening theme, the second subject is less continuous, and consists of shorter phrases. In the short but very concentrated development, the main theme appears against a new and menacing figure which also appears in the recapitulation and, still more, in the very powerful and dramatic coda. This rises to a climax of great intensity, with an almost orchestral texture; both this and the very pathetic final bars have a strongly romantic flavour.

To find the right sequel to so emotional a movement might well have caused Beethoven some hesitation. In the D major Piano Sonata from Op 10, the very tragic slow movement is followed by a lyrical minuet that supplies exactly the right feeling of consolation. After the equally eloquent Adagio in Op 18, No 1 the Scherzo that follows it does, on first hearing at least, seem rather brittle and impersonal. But in itself it is an admirable and very individual movement. The sketches are interesting; originally the first section was to contain only eight bars, ending with a more conventional cadence, while the second began with a couple of two-bar phrases. Eventually the first eight bars were extended to ten, with shorter phrases and a more capricious style; the second section as it stands begins very effectively with two phrases of three bars. At the end the device of postponing the final cadence for as long as possible is carried to still greater lengths than in the third movement of the D major Quartet. The general mood of this Scherzo is rather like that of the so-called Minuet in the first symphony, but it is more subtle and light-footed. The Trio is highly characteristic and original, with a grotesquely leaping figure alternating with rapid scale passages; the tonality shifts constantly, and when it eventually swings round to the dominant it arrives a beat earlier than is expected, in a manner sometimes deprecated by textbooks but often to be found in Beethoven's later works.

The Finale is an interesting and eventful movement with a

good deal more in it than its rather flippant opening might
suggest. It is in rondo form, planned on a large scale, as can
be felt at once from the length of the main subject, and the very
leisurely way in which it moves to the dominant for the first
episode. The themes are varied in character; the rhythm of the
first is as well marked as that of the main theme of the first
Allegro, but it does not dominate the whole movement in the
same way. The most striking feature of this Finale is the
development of the quiet cadential theme:

Ex 3

which first appears at the end of the first episode. In the central
episode it is introduced in a different form, with more slowly
moving harmony, alternating with a fugal passage based on the
main theme, and appearing in a variety of keys. The same
procedure was employed by Beethoven on several later occasions, including the Rondo of the 'Emperor' Concerto and
also, on a vast scale, by Schubert in the first movement of the
C major String Quintet. In the coda an entirely new phrase is
introduced, with admirable effect, as a counterpoint to the
first theme. All through the quartet the interest is most skilfully divided between the players, and the texture varies greatly
—for the most part it is very clear, but sometimes, especially
in the Adagio, remarkably rich.

   The Quartet in G major is less ambitious and less varied in
content, but it is a work of great beauty and gaiety. Its opening
is as different as possible from that of the F major; instead of
a single, persistently developed theme there is a series of
phrases that have no obvious connection with each other but
make a very delightful and convincing sentence. In the exposition there are no great contrasts of mood, but ideas follow

each other cheerfully, the opening of the second subject being a light-hearted relation of the Adagio of the 'Pathetic' Sonata. A cadential phrase from the first theme ends the exposition and opens the development—a procedure common in Beethoven's work. The most striking feature of the development is a fugal passage built on a phrase from the first subject; it is marked 'sempre pianissimo', and Beethoven is clearly using a fugal texture to produce an atmosphere of tension and mystery, just as Haydn did in the fugal finales of some of the Op 20 quartets. And with both composers the tension is eventually resolved into something loud and homophonic. The return of the first subject after the development is delightfully contrived: it appears in a much more aggressive mood than before, against a background of marching quavers, the first four bars being played first by the cello and then repeated by the first violin. The coda is shorter than that of the first movements of the quartets in F and D, but it is perfectly suited to the general mood of the movement and ends with a charming reminiscence of the first subject.

The first theme of the Adagio took Beethoven some time to evolve; in his sketch-books there are several versions in common time including the following:

Ex 4

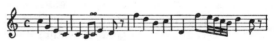

This also foreshadows the melodic line of the eventual version in triple time:

Ex 5

and might possibly have still been in Beethoven's mind when, a few years later, he wrote the song 'Die Ehre Gottes aus der Natur'.

Ex 6

There is some ornate decorative writing not unlike that in the slow movement of Mozart's K. 387 in the same key. Beethoven's texture is less subtle and varied than that of the Mozart movement, but it is massive and dignified and contrasts vividly with the quick central section. This is a very unusual feature for the period, especially in a chamber work, but Haydn had provided something like a precedent in the very curious slow Finale of his Quartet in C major, Op 54, No 2. Beethoven himself, in the Serenade, Op 8, had written an Adagio interrupted twice by a Scherzo, and later, in the Piano Sonata in E♭ major, Op 27, No 1 he was to write a slow first movement with a quick central episode. In the Adagio of the Quartet in G major the theme of the central section is ingeniously derived from the preceding cadential phrase. When it has run its course, the theme of the first section returns very impressively in the bass; in the coda the touches of F minor have a curiously nostalgic effect characteristic of the nineteenth rather than the eighteenth century.

The Scherzo has points in common with that of the A major Piano Sonata from Op 2, the main themes of the two being decidedly similar. The quartet movement, however, is longer and considerably more elaborate in its texture; its good humour is more unclouded, and has not the suggestion of gruffness that is to be found in the earlier one. The Trio opens in a deceptively demure manner, but becomes increasingly high-spirited as it proceeds. It is followed by a transitional passage leading to the *da capo*, in which the bass moves slowly and deliberately down the scale under reminiscences of the theme of the Scherzo; the effect is strangely impressive, especially in its light-hearted surroundings. This Scherzo is not, perhaps, quite as bold and original as that of the F major Quartet, but it is a most delightful movement which fits perfectly into the generally gay atmosphere of the whole work. The Finale is in full sonata form without repeat. It has great vivacity, and it is therefore rather surprising to find that in the early sketches the note values were twice as long, giving the music an entirely different aspect. Its mood is decidedly like that of some of Haydn's and Mozart's livelier finales in 2/4 time, and the impressive modulation to F near the end of the exposition recalls passages at similar moments in the finales of Mozart's C major Quartet, K. 465, and Quintet, K. 515. But it has many characteristic features; especially perhaps the hammering insistence on the chord of D major at the end of the exposition, which is oddly prophetic of a passage in Mendelssohn's *Midsummer Night's Dream* overture. Finer still is a passage towards the end of the development where there is a similar insistence on the chord of the dominant minor ninth, but this time in a brooding and mysterious atmosphere, leading quite unexpectedly to a very remote key. A comparison between this movement and the first movement of Schubert's Violin Sonata in D major is of interest. The main themes of the two movements are rhythmically identical, but otherwise they are completely unlike; Schubert's, for once in a way, is more concise than Beethoven's, and is in a flowing lyrical mood far removed from Beethoven's high spirits. Of all the Op 18 quartets the G major comes nearest to the eighteenth century in its urbanity. But, without attaining to the profundity of the greatest works of Haydn and Mozart, it can stand firmly on its own feet as a most delightful and refreshing work, in no way inferior to its bolder and more forward-looking companions.

The Quartet in C minor is the most vigorous of the six and makes the most direct appeal. With Beethoven C minor is usually the key for drama and tension; the first movement of this quartet has its dramatic moments, but the main thematic material is flowing and lyrical, the opening of the second subject being derived, perhaps subconsciously, from the fifth bar of the first. Both themes are allowed to proceed in a broad and leisurely way; if this movement is compared with the first movements of Mozart's String Quartet in D minor, or String Quintet in G minor, by both of which it was probably influenced, it can be seen at once that it is less subtle and concentrated and its rhetoric perhaps more obvious. But it has a fine spaciousness and geniality and moments of great power, especially in the coda, where a quiet transitional theme from the exposition appears in an unexpectedly menacing mood. In both the development and the coda Beethoven shows great resource in presenting his themes with new counterpoints or new harmonic backgrounds. Despite its dark-coloured opening and passionate close, this movement is less predominantly stormy than the first movements of some of the other works in this key, such as the String Trio and the Violin Sonata. But it is richer and more massive in texture than those of the other Op 18 quartets.

This is the first of several works by Beethoven that contain both a scherzo and a minuet but no slow movement. In this case the Scherzo is marked no faster than 'Andante scherzoso quasi Allegretto', but it is light and playful in mood and very similar in form and texture to the second movement of the slightly earlier first symphony. Both of these combine sonata form with a certain amount of fugal writing and in this movement the fugal element is more prominent. It is not, however,

B

entirely orthodox; in the exposition it is pleasant to see
Beethoven writing an answer which would be marked down
severely in an examination and also committing the solecism
of having two successive entries beginning on the same degree
of the scale. The fugal texture is not kept up throughout the
movement, but as in certain movements by Mozart the changes
from a contrapuntal to a harmonic texture are carried out with
delightful ease. In both this and the first movement the transitional passage draws up on the dominant and this is followed,
not by the second subject but by a few bars that lead to the
necessary key. The second subject itself is not fugal but contains enough canonic writing to bring it into line with the rest
of the movement, and towards the end of the exposition the
three repeated notes of the opening theme are constantly recalled. The development begins contrapuntally, but its most
impressive feature is a passage of quiet harmonic suspense,
still dominated by the three repeated notes, in which the music
shows every sign of being about to go to A minor and then at
the last minute changes its mind and returns to C major for
the recapitulation. This opens with a fascinating orgy of triple
counterpoint; the coda looks back for a moment to the end of
the development, after which the first theme makes its final
appearance, not contrapuntally but as a kind of waltz. The part
played by counterpoint in Beethoven's works is very varied;
sometimes, especially in late works, he used it to express a
tense and tortured emotion, such as is found also in some of
Mozart's fugues. But here it is used lightly and gracefully for
a delicate comedy of manners worthy of Jane Austen.

In the works where Beethoven has both scherzo and minuet
the latter is usually placid and lyrical, as in the Piano Sonata
in E♭ major, Op 31, No 3. In this quartet, however, it is surprisingly sombre and passionate. Even in the first four bars
the tonality is curiously restless and this feeling is increased by
the constant *sforzandi* on the third beat of the bar. There is a

suggestion of Mozart in the chromaticisms in the second part, but they are more intense and there is a strong foretaste of Schubert in the modulation to D♭. The Trio, which is for the most part a dialogue between the second violin and viola, is rather more conventional, especially in the elegant cadences at the end of each half, but it is delightfully scored, and its leisurely harmonic motion is eminently characteristic of Beethoven. After this peaceful interlude the *da capo* of the Minuet, which is directed to be played faster than before, is curiously disquieting and emphasises still more the strikingly restless character of the movement. The Finale, like that of the D major Quartet, is rather more Haydnesque than the rest of the work. It is a rondo, very clear-cut and sectional in its form but extremely varied in its content. The lively main theme recurs many times, often with some variation of either melody or texture. The melody of the first episode is given to the second violin, which has a particularly grateful part throughout the Quartet; its first few notes are echoed with charming effect by the first violin:

Ex 7

The second episode is gruff and very terse; the return of the main theme leads to a long and eventful coda. The melody of the first episode returns, sounding very serene and ethereal in C major; the main theme undergoes a series of adventures, after which it makes it last complete appearance *prestissimo*. But instead of the expected climax Beethoven appears to have the intention of ending quietly in the major, as he had done in several earlier works in the same key (the Piano Trio, the String Trio and the Piano Sonata, Op 10, No 1). At the last moment, however, he changes his mind, and ends with a loud and sudden reminiscence of the gruff central episode. Thayer's theory that this is the latest in date of the six quartets is not supported by factual evidence; and with all its fine qualities, it is no more mature than certain things in the others. But it is surprising that no sketches for it have survived.

3

Op 18 (continued)

IF the Quartet in C minor is the most forceful of the six, the fifth, in A major, is the quietest and most retiring. It has strong affinities with Mozart's quartet in the same key, K. 464, which in all probability served as a model. But the two first movements are in many ways very unalike; Mozart's is very closely knit and economical with its material, while Beethoven's is far more capricious and wanders in a pleasant, light-hearted way from one idea to another. Now and again the texture is so bare as to suggest that of the posthumous quartets:

Ex 8

The transitional passage draws up ceremoniously on the dominant in a way which by that time was slightly archaic, but the second subject follows, as in the Piano Sonata Op 2, No 3, in the dominant minor with admirable effect. The counterpoint is lively, and, compared with that in the Mozart movement, more brittle and less smooth in sound. The development flows easily and vivaciously, but its most distinguished moment is when the expected return to the main theme is held up for a few moments by a quietly ruminating passage. The short coda, in which the first violin seems at one point to be half a bar behind the others, is particularly effective if the repeat of the second half has been played.

The Minuet, coming second, seems at first sight to be very naïve and simple, especially when compared to the remarkably subtle and closely wrought Minuet from Mozart's Quartet in A major. But its easy tunefulness conceals much skilful and delightful workmanship, especially in its texture. The two-part writing at the beginning suggests Haydn rather than Mozart; when it returns after the abrupt cadence in C♯ minor (one of the few *fortissimo* moments in the work), the series of imitations and the gradual amplification of sound are beautifully contrived, and the last eight bars round the movement off perfectly. The melody of the Trio is one of the five passages in Beethoven's music that recall the melody of the slow movement of Haydn's Symphony No 88. But it is very dangerous to attach too much importance to thematic resemblances of this kind, especially in music written at a time when there were so many familiar turns of phrase used by all and sundry. Haydn's tune is slow and majestic, and Beethoven's recollections of it all move at a quicker pace, sometimes with the suggestion of a dance. Even in the first movement of the A♭ major Piano Sonata, Op 110, where the melody moves with greater breadth and deliberation, the atmosphere is very different from that of Haydn's movement. In the Trio of the Minuet of Beethoven's Quartet in A the tune is given a new character by *sforzandi* on the third beats of several bars. This here produces, not the restless effect of the Minuet of the C minor Quartet, but a feeling of comfortable conviviality, which is further emphasised by the doubling of the melody in octaves. To return for a moment to the Minuet itself, it would be interesting to know whether its first phrase was unconsciously in Beethoven's head when, twenty-six years later, he wrote the 'Es muß sein' theme in his Op 135.

The third movement is a set of variations on a theme which in its original sketch began as follows:

Ex 9

The rest of the sketch is more like the eventual version, but the alteration of the first four bars is drastic and results in a simpler and more dignified melodic line with a less repetitive harmonic basis. There is an obvious parallel between this movement and the variations in Mozart's Quartet in A major, but in many ways the two sets are very dissimilar. On the whole Mozart set himself the harder problem, as his theme is richer in detail, both melodic and harmonic, than that of Beethoven, and proportionately harder to vary. He keeps close to the original harmonic outline in his variations, but they have a wealth of new melodies that are so attractive and spontaneous that, hearing them away from their context, one would hardly guess them to be variations of another tune. Beethoven keeps far more closely to the simple melodic outline of his theme and obtains his contrasts by variations of texture which are perhaps more obvious than those of Mozart, but very effective. The first variation is light-heartedly fugal and the second a lively *pas seul* for the first violin. In the third there is a new and attractive luxuriance of colour and the cadence at the end of the first half, where the bass moves a beat later than is expected, is prophetic of later things. In the fourth the melody is simplified and the harmony varied; at the beginning of the second half the change from F♯ minor to a dominant seventh on D is remarkably beautiful. After the robust comedy of the fifth, the modulation to B♭ for the coda is magical. Curiously enough the new melody that enters as a counterpoint to the theme had been sketched some years before for a Piano Rondo in C minor. The gradual return to the key of D and the final reminiscences of the theme are beautifully contrived.

The Finale, again, has points in common with that of Mozart's Quartet in A, and in this case the differences are less pronounced. Both movements combine sonata form with a good deal of free contrapuntal writing and both end quietly. But again, Mozart's movement is the more closely knit; the only moment of contrast comes with the fleeting appearance of a chorale-like melody in the development. Beethoven obtains his contrast with his second subject, which is a kind of augmentation of a tune that had already been used in a barer and more contrapuntal texture in the Finale of the 'Pathetic' Sonata. The development contains the most powerful passage in the work, which is followed by a delightful variation of the second subject. In a sketch of the opening bars, the imitations of the little phrase of four notes appear over a harmonic accompaniment which would have contributed little and could easily have spoilt the clear texture of the music.

The Quartet in A, moving quietly within a comparatively narrow range, is a very unified and convincing whole. The sixth, in B♭ major, larger, more varied and more ambitious, leaves a less satisfactory impression, owing to its odd diversity of styles. The first movement is superficially Haydnesque in manner. The material is lightweight, but without the underlying profundity of many similar movements by Haydn, and Beethoven does not here show the capacity for seeing unexpected possibilities in apparently trivial themes that is so marked in such a movement as the Finale of the Piano Sonata in E♭ major, Op 31, No 3. Though pleasantly vivacious, this is on the whole the least interesting of the six first movements, and its most attractive features are not so much the main thematic ideas as the incidental touches, such as the modulations in the second subject and the passage at the end of the development:

Ex 10

Allegro con brio

which seems to have no thematic connection with anything else in the movement, but supplies a charming touch of poetry in comparatively prosaic surroundings. The scale passages that first appear shortly before the second subject give rise to some lively imitative writing during the development, but, with all its energy, the general impression left by this movement is rather impersonal and undistinguished.

The slow movement has a gentle and leisurely elegance and is remarkable more for the varied and resourceful texture of the string-writing than for its thematic material. The main theme, rather naïve in itself, is decorated in various ways, sometimes rhythmic and sometimes contrapuntal, which give it a different character every time it recurs. The much barer and more sombre texture of the central section makes a very impressive contrast; when it is recalled in the coda it leads to a modulation which is undoubtedly the finest moment in the movement. But the Scherzo which follows has considerably more character and originality. The constant cross-rhythms shifting between 3/4 and 6/8, commoner at certain earlier and later periods, were far from usual in 1800, and here they are made to sound especially eccentric owing to frequent *sforzandi* on the last quaver of the bar. Towards the end there is an exhilarating climax followed by an abrupt collapse. This is comedy of a far rougher and more wilful kind than the good-humoured gaiety of the Quartet in G; it looks ahead to later works and must have sounded very disconcerting to contemporary audiences. The Trio is still rather capricious, but less aggressive; it is followed however by four bars in B♭ minor which recall the cross-rhythm of the Scherzo in a highly indignant manner, and lead to the *da capo*.

The first three movements of this quartet, taken as a whole, give the impression that the composer, beginning at a comparatively low level of inspiration, seems to gather strength as the work proceeds. The Adagio, though not one of the finest of Beethoven's early slow movements, is superior to the lively but rather superficial first movement, and the Scherzo is robustly and defiantly individual. The slow introduction of the Finale is still more remarkable; it is entitled 'La Malinconia' and, as in the Adagio of No 1, the unusually elaborate directions suggest that Beethoven was conscious of writing in an unusually emotional style. It opens with a phrase of great beauty which could, if required, have grown into a full-sized slow movement. But Beethoven was sometimes strangely severe on his own ideas. Such phrases as the opening of the Piano Sonata in F♯ major, or the second subject of the first movement of the Quartet in B♭ major, Op 130, could well have been allowed to expand into long melodies, but Beethoven instead preferred to leave them as hints rather than statements. The opening phrase of 'La Malinconia' is treated more extensively, but the treatment is harmonic, not melodic, and soon an unexpected modulation leads to a keyless succession of diminished sevenths:

Ex 11

Beethoven is said to have admitted to a pupil that 'the startling effects which many ascribe solely to the natural genius of the composer are frequently easily achieved by the right use and application of the chord of the diminished seventh'. But he would probably have been the first to admit that this particular chord can easily cloy, especially in a succession rising or falling by semitones. In this passage the effect is very striking: the group of three grace notes derives from the previous phrase, and the contrasts of colour and dynamics have a strong feeling of tension. After a passage of much barer texture the group of grace notes becomes increasingly insistent; eventually it rises very impressively by semitones in the bass and there is a pause on the dominant of B♭. The whole passage, if scored for full orchestra, would hardly sound out of place in a mature work by Wagner.

The idea of following a mysterious chromatic introduction by a cheerful quick movement may have been suggested to Beethoven by Mozart's Quartet in C major, K. 465. It poses a problem which Mozart, writing at the height of his powers, could solve perfectly; the very strange introduction to his quartet heightens the beauty of the lyrical first theme of the Allegro. But Beethoven, in this curiously transitional work, could not succeed in the same way. His Finale is a lively movement of considerable charm, but, after the extraordinary harmonic adventures of the introduction, it seems to be a disconcerting throwback to a different and more conventional world. An early sketch of its main theme:

Ex 12

shows that in its original form it had more similarity to the theme of the Finale of the Piano Sonata in D minor. It is in an unusual form, a kind of rondo in which the second episode is a recapitulation of the first; Schubert and Bruckner were both fond of it, especially for slow movements. Shortly before the last return of the theme, the opening phrase of the introduction is twice recalled and the first four bars of the main theme are played in a slow tempo just before the very rapid coda, a procedure that reappears in the Rondo of the G major Piano Sonata, Op 31, No 1. The Quartet in B♭ as a whole leaves a curiously mixed impression, but it is possible that Beethoven may have meant it to be the climax of the set. It covers a wide range, and the Scherzo and the introduction to the Finale are as enterprising and original as anything that he had written at that time. But there is a strange diversity between the movements, not only in merit but also in idiom, as a result of which it remains a highly interesting but unsatisfying work.

The fact that emerges most obviously from a survey of these six works is that Beethoven was already a master of the problems of writing for string quartet. The fugal passages, in whatever mood, are always successful and he has fully realised that a contrapuntal texture need not necessarily be fugal, or even imitative. The slow movements of Mozart's Quartet in C major, K. 465, or of Haydn's Quartet in F major, Op 77, No 2, would be sufficient to stamp both composers as great contrapuntists, even if they had neither of them written a note of fugue. Without rising to this supremely high level several movements in Beethoven's Op 18 show the same feeling for lyrical, non-fugal counterpoint—especially the Andante of the Quartet in D major and the Adagio of the Quartet in B♭ major, in both of which the texture and development are more interesting than the material. The increasingly frequent use of *sforzando* that is so characteristic of Beethoven's early piano sonatas can be seen in the quartets also. Sometimes it gives an unexpected jolt to an otherwise placid tune, such as that of the Trio of the Minuet of the Quartet in A major, or the Finale of the Quartet in B♭ major; more often it leads to a rhetoric more emphatic and vehement than that of Haydn or Mozart. The six works all have their own individual character, those in F major and C minor giving on the whole the most complete picture of the composer. Both of them contrive to cover a wide range of mood without the stylistic uncertainty and inconsistency that spoils the Quartet in B♭ despite its remarkable features. The other three are in their different ways strongly unified, especially perhaps the G major. Of the other instrumental works dating from this period, the Piano Sonata in B♭ major, Op 22, is the one that has most in common with the Op 18 quartets. Its Adagio is less poignant than that of the Quartet in F, but the two movements, both in 9/8 time, have the same mixture of flowing Italianate melody with rich and nostalgic harmony of a more Teutonic kind. The other movements of the sonata, in all of which a smooth exterior conceals undercurrents of suspense and unrest, are akin to several movements from Op 18. At this stage Beethoven is not in the mood for the heroics of the 'Pathetic' Sonata, or the richly emotional outpourings of some of the earlier slow movements; but in Op 22 and Op 18 he is able to use an idiom that is in no way revolutionary, but has far more independence and imagination than several more externally ambitious works of the same period, such as the Septet and the first symphony.

In 1802 Beethoven, observing with disapproval the popularity of transcription, gave a demonstration of how it should be done by making an arrangement for string quartet of his Piano Sonata in E major, Op 14, No 1. This is done with great freedom and sensitiveness, though the process is not as drastic as the remodelling of the Octet for wind instruments as a string quintet, which becomes virtually a new and more interesting work. The sonata is transposed from E to F, and the tempi of the first and last movements are altered, that of the former being changed from Allegro to Allegro moderato and that of the latter from Allegro comodo to Allegro. The texture of

the quartet version is lighter and clearer; at the beginning of
the central Allegretto, for instance, there is no attempt to
emulate the rich sound of the piano. On the other hand, in the
long pedal point that prepares the way for the second subject
of the first movement a suggestion of counterpoint in the
original is far more fully realised in the transcription. But it is
in the Finale that the texture is most drastically altered, as can
be seen at once from the opening bars:

Ex 13

and in the central episode Beethoven keeps the harmonic outline unchanged but completely alters the texture; the purely

pianistic arpeggios of the original give place to an entirely different figuration, in which running passages in triplets are ingeniously combined with a cadential phrase from the main theme. Apart from its containing only three movements, there is nothing to indicate that it is an arrangement. In certain ways the character of the work has been changed; the subdued, rather wistful lyricism of the sonata has been turned into something rather more precise and clear-cut, but the result is very delightful and well worth enjoying in its own right, apart from the extraordinary skill with which it has been done.

4

Op 59

SIX years separated the composition of Op 18 from that of
Op 59. At first sight the gulf between them seems immensely
wide, and except for No 3 their first reception was far from
favourable. But a study of the intervening works shows how
gradual was the development of Beethoven's style during the
early years of the nineteenth century. He himself described the
three piano sonatas, Op 31, as being in a new style and the
sombre rhetorical splendour of the Sonata in D minor from
this group and the Sonata for violin and piano in C minor from
Op 30 is perhaps the most obviously new and powerful side of
his personality. But on the whole it was to find fuller expression
in piano and orchestral music, and there are other features,
equally characteristic, that play a more important part in the
development of Beethoven's style in his quartets. On the one
hand there is the odd, rather enigmatic abruptness to be found,
for instance, in the first two movements of the Piano Sonata
in E♭ major, Op 27, No 1; on the other, the flowing spaciousness of the first movements of the String Quintet in C major,
Op 29 and the Piano Sonata in D major, Op 28. These were
both written in 1801 and during the following years Beethoven
produced a large number of masterpieces of astonishingly
diverse character. Sometimes, as in the first movements of the
third and fifth symphonies, he was concerned with building
large structures on short but pregnant themes, with only passing suggestions of lyricism. But the rich flowing beauty of the

slow movements of the Violin Sonata in A major from Op 30 and the fourth symphony show that Beethoven had fully retained his love of melody, often of a simpler and more direct kind than in his earlier works. It has already been suggested that the string quartet could not have been a suitable medium for the tremendously vehement emotion that is expressed in some of the works of Beethoven's second period. Nor would it be congenial to the virtuosity of the 'Kreutzer' and 'Waldstein' Sonatas. Compared with other works written at the same time, the 'Rasumovsky' Quartets seem in some ways to steer a middle course; this can be felt at once if we put the sombre passion of the first movement of the second quartet beside that of the 'Appassionata' Sonata, or the brilliance of the Finale of the third quartet beside that of the 'Waldstein' Sonata. But they are far richer and more varied in texture than any of the earlier quartets, and their size, especially that of the first quartet, is of truly symphonic spaciousness.

At the request of Count Rasumovsky, Beethoven expressed his intention of introducing Russian folksongs into all three quartets; eventually he did it only in the first two, and his treatment of the tunes is decidedly high-handed. He wrote them both down in a sketch-book, marking one 'Molto Andante' and the other 'Andante', but eventually introduced them at a far brisker pace, regardless of the fact that one tells of a soldier prematurely aged by the rigours of military life, and the other is a hymn of praise to God. As presented by Beethoven in the quartets they seem, perhaps, slightly more rustic than is usual in his style, but certainly no more than some of the tunes in the 'Pastoral' Symphony; the theme used in the Finale of the first quartet is admirably suited for development and its ambiguous tonality has parallels in other works. The spaciousness that is so characteristic of Op 59 as a whole is particularly noticeable in No 1 and most of all in its first movement, which is one of Beethoven's most impressive

achievements. Here, following in the footsteps of the String
Quintet and the Op 28 Piano Sonata, he builds, not upon short
incisive figures but on flowing and continuous melodies that
are capable of being divided at a later stage into smaller,
separable units. The first movements of the Violin Concerto,
the Cello Sonata in A major, Op 69, and the Piano Trio in B♭
major, Op 97 are equally fine instances. The opening of Op 59,
No 1 is remarkable for many reasons. The well-known theme:

Ex 14

is strong both rhythmically and melodically, and during the
exposition it gives rise to various offshoots:

Ex 15

Ex 16

Ex 17

which all come from the same source, but all have their own individual character. Equally striking is the way in which the opening tune is played first under and then above repeated chords, the harmony changing seldom and not always at the most likely moment. This combination of slow harmonic motion and rhythmic energy is very characteristic of Beethoven; it appears, in a more turbulent mood and with less melodic interest, in the opening of the 'Waldstein' Sonata, and, in a more serene and Olympian atmosphere, in the first movement of the B♭ major Piano Trio, Op 97. In the first movement of Op 59, No 1 the second subject is as flowing and melodious as the first, but there are contrasting elements in the exposition, such as the well-marked rhythmic figure that occurs quite early in the movement and the very curious passage:

Ex 18

which casts a mysterious shadow and looks ahead to the bare colouring of the posthumous quartets. The exposition ends quietly with Ex 17, which is very happily placed; its second and third bars recall the opening theme of the movement and the quavers in the fourth bar look ahead to important later developments.

It is characteristic of the great continuity of this movement that there should be no double-bar and repeat at the end of the exposition. This had already happened in the first movements of two slightly earlier works, the Violin Sonata in C minor from Op 30 and the 'Appassionata'. In the former instance the very impressive entry of the first theme in the relative major at the end of the exposition makes a repeat quite impossible and in the latter the exposition ends in A♭ minor, from which it would be highly inconvenient to return to F minor, the tonic, for a repeat. But here the effect is quite different; the exposition leads quietly to the first theme in the tonic, making a feint at a repeat. This procedure recurs several times in the music of Brahms, notably in the first movements of his Piano Quartet in G minor and fourth symphony; it inevitably needs to be followed by a long and eventful development. In the present instance, the theme soon moves away into other keys and eventually the quavers in its second and third bars break away from the rest and indulge in a heated argument, which is dispersed quietly by the mysterious chords of Ex 18. The passage that follows is one of the finest in the work. The opening phrase of the movement is expanded by the first violin into a long-drawn meditation over sustained harmonies, the music modulating very deliberately and impressively into D♭. Gradually the other parts become less static; Ex 14 turns almost imperceptibly into Ex 17, and the quavers of its fourth bar are soon involved in a fugal development against an entirely new theme. This does not continue for long, however, and the music returns nearer home; for a moment Ex 17 appears in the dominant, as it did in the exposition. But the expected recapitulation does not come for some time; a graceful triplet figure that had previously appeared during the course of the second group is worked against two bars from Ex 14 (or 17) leading to a rising passage over a dominant pedal which would certainly suggest a *crescendo* if Beethoven had not marked it *sempre piano*. All now seems set for the return of the main theme, but instead comes the vigorous rhythmic phrase that followed it in the exposition. A series of diminished sevenths produces a feeling of harmonic suspense and, at long last, the first theme returns very unceremoniously in the bass, without being heralded by the usual dominant harmony, and the recapitulation begins.

The whole course of the development is wonderfully planned; it is resourceful, imaginative and full of the carefully graded and controlled tension that is characteristic of the whole movement. In the recapitulation the first theme soon plunges into an exciting digression to D♭, the opening of the second group has a more animated accompaniment, and the harmonies of Ex 18 are made slightly more shadowy by the alteration of a semitone. But the climax of the movement comes at the beginning of the coda when, after a quick *crescendo*, the first theme is played in a high register by the first violin, over rich and massive block harmony. The effect of this is overwhelming and set a problem to the composer; it would be difficult to follow without an anticlimax, while on the other-hand too brief a conclusion would be out of character with the broad scale on which the movement is constructed. Beethoven's solution is leisurely and spacious; for some time the first phrase of the main theme is treated imitatively against a background of triplets, with alternating tonic and dominant harmonies. Particularly striking, therefore, is the effect of the chord of D minor that comes first before the final cadence.

At this stage of Beethoven's career it is unusual for a scherzo to appear as the second movement; the most notable instances are the Cello Sonata in A major, the Piano Trio in B♭ major, Op 97, and the present quartet, in all of which the first movements are particularly broad and melodious in character. A far more uncommon feature of the quartet is the fact that all four movements, including the Scherzo, are in full sonata form. Mendelssohn's 'Scottish' Symphony seems to be the only other familiar instance, though there are one or two border-line cases among his chamber works. Seldom has the form been treated with so much elaborate detail and yet with so light a touch as in the second movement of this quartet. The dialogue with which it begins, regarded as wildly inconsequent by

Beethoven's contemporaries, has a subtle and imaginative tonal scheme. The change from F to A♭:

Ex 19

gives a sense of mystery which is heightened eight bars later by another change from E♭ to C♭, after which the music quietly returns to the tonic for a charmingly contrasted lyrical phrase. The exposition is packed with ideas; what appears at first sight to be the second subject leads merely to a return to the main key for yet another theme:

Ex 20

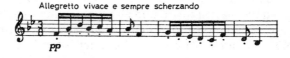

which proves to be the most haunting in the movement. Eventually the second subject arrives in the dominant minor, and unexpectedly melancholy. But this mood is prevented from luxuriating by the bustling semiquavers that become more and more insistent during the latter part of the exposition and continue almost uninterrupted during the development, stopping

only occasionally, either for a moment of lyrical relief or for
a dramatic pause. This development is eventful and broadly
designed; there are some fine instances of Beethoven's favourite
combination of rhythmic energy and slowly moving harmony
and there are two new ideas, both derived from the opening
bar of the movement:

Ex 21

Ex 22

The second of these leads to the recapitulation; this begins not
with the opening dialogue but with the quiet lyrical theme that
followed it. Apart from two mysterious intrusions of Ex 22 in
an unexpectedly bleak guise the recapitulation is regular. In
the coda the opening dialogue, which had been omitted in the
recapitulation, is brought back in an amplified form, the
melody of Ex 22 being used as a counterpoint to the first four
bars. In the last page there is a strange digression in which the
lyrical theme appears for a moment in a very remote key;
finally the movement ends with Beethoven's favourite juxtaposition of *pianissimo* and *fortissimo*. In no part of his output
is he more versatile than in his scherzos and this is one of his
most individual. Its mood had been mildly foreshadowed in

the Andante scherzoso from Op 18, No 4, and, far more vividly, in the delightful Allegretto vivace Scherzo from the Piano Sonata, Op 31, No 3; both of these are in sonata form. The piano movement has the same bustle of semiquavers, but it is squarer and more earth-bound; in the quartet movement the abundance of varied ideas and the beautiful touches of lyricism give it a peculiar sensitiveness and poetry. Its influence can be felt in many of Mendelssohn's scherzos, though none of them have quite the same variety or subtlety of organisation.

The increasingly wide choice of keys for the central movements of works suggests that Beethoven was very sensitive to the relations between the last chord of one movement and the first of the next. In Op 59, No 1 the key of the Scherzo, B♭ major, is unusual, and after its loud and triumphant end the opening of the Adagio sounds particularly desolate. The main theme is preceded by an unaccompanied middle C played by the second violin and enters over a bare fifth. The sketches of the melody are less unlike the final version than is often the case with Beethoven, but Ex 23 shows how much less continuous was the original form:

Ex 23

In the next version the demisemiquaver passage was omitted and the continuation of the melody was very similar to the final version, but the fourth bar still retained its rather pedestrian character, and in bar 8 there was a full close, followed by a repetition of the melody by the cello. Eventually bar 4 was much improved by a very simple change, and a half close at bar 8 greatly enhanced the repetition of the melody by the cello. The passage as it now stands is one of Beethoven's finest; the melody has great distinction and the counterpoint played by the first violin from bar 9 onwards is equally beautiful.

Underneath a wealth of expressive detail the form of the movement is basically simple. A transition that grows imperceptibly from the last bar of the first theme leads to the second subject which, as so often in slow movements in sonata form, is less long-breathed than the first. Beginning with short and simple phrases based on tonic and dominant:

Ex 24

it rises quickly to a powerful climax which is followed by a quiet and haunting cadential phrase. All these things happen with a kind of 'majestic instancy', the whole passage being only six bars longer than the long-drawn melody of the first subject. So far the music has been continuously in minor keys and the change to the relative major at the beginning of the development is deeply moving. It is worth noting that it is the more unassuming second subject that is used at this juncture; the first theme, transposed to the major, would have lost terribly in stature. Though not particularly long, this development is rich and eventful; phrases from the first subject are treated imitatively, and eventually the cadential figure that appeared at the end of the exposition seems to be leading inexorably towards the recapitulation. Instead, however, it moves quietly into Db major, where a new melody appears. This is a moment of extraordinary beauty, but Beethoven characteristically does not allow the tune to luxuriate in such a way as to hold up the action. It is punctuated by the rhythm of the cadential phrase, just as, in the first movement of the fifth symphony, the lyrical second theme is held firmly in check by the menacing rhythm of the opening phrase. Before long the music returns to F minor and the recapitulation begins. The first theme is curtailed from sixteen to eight bars and the harmonic background is more agitated; the transition is also curtailed, involving a wistful glance back towards D♭ major. The coda begins with a final return of the main theme, very richly scored, but it is not allowed to finish, and eventually the movement runs straight into the Finale.

This happens quite frequently during this period of Beethoven's life, but with varying results. Sometimes, as in the 'Appassionata', the Violin Concerto and the 'Archduke' Trio, a mood of particular serenity is abruptly swept aside by a sudden dramatic stroke. Sometimes, on the other hand, it happens with far more deliberation, as in the long-drawn *crescendo* that leads from the Scherzo to the Finale of the fifth symphony, or the equally gradual *diminuendo* at the end of the storm movement in the 'Pastoral' Symphony. In Op 59, No 1 the transition from the slow movement to the Finale is on similar lines, though on a smaller scale; the harmonic movement becomes increasingly slow and over a sustained dominant seventh the first violin plays a long florid passage leading into the Finale. For so deeply felt and tragic a movement it is a surprising outcome. A few years later Beethoven pursued a similar course in the Piano Sonata in E♭ major, Op 81a, but there the mood of the Andante is elegiac rather than tragic and its gentle pathos could be dispelled comparatively easily. But in the Adagio of the F major Quartet, with its far more sombre colouring, emphasised by the unusual direction *mesto*, only a very broad and gradual dispelling of the tragic mood would have been possible without a feeling of anticlimax; the florid passage for the first violin, in itself quite undistinguished, provides in its context the necessary feeling of suspense before the opening of the Finale. Before we leave this movement mention should be made, if only for the sake of completeness, of the cryptic phrase 'a weeping willow or acacia over the grave of my brother', written after one of the sketches of the main theme. That Beethoven should have been thinking of his brother Georg, who had died in infancy, is just possible though unlikely; the other suggested explanation, that it was a lament for the marriage of his brother Karl, of which he strongly disapproved, seems even more far-fetched.

After so magnificent a slow movement the Finale leaves a somewhat impersonal impression, despite its brilliance and energy. It is admirably constructed; the 'translated' Russian folk-tune is treated with great resource and the second group contains two contrasted elements, one lyrical and the other rhythmic. The first of these is not allowed to make more than a fleeting impression; for a brief moment it casts a shadow over the picture when it appears canonically in the minor. The other has immense drive and plays a very important part in the development. There are several interesting structural features in the movement: the long cadenza-like passage for the first violin that preceded it is twice recalled, first at the end of the exposition and later during the development; the return of the main theme for the recapitulation is cunningly and subtly contrived, with the tune pretending to be in the wrong key; and in the coda there is some very neat and lively fugal writing. Just before the end, after an exciting climax, Beethoven, remembering perhaps the elegiac character of the folk-tune in its original form, presents it in a slow tempo, over gently nostalgic harmonies, but, as so often, this is soon brushed aside with much vigour.

The spacious, almost symphonic character of this quartet has already been stressed; equally remarkable is its variety. After the full, rich texture of the first movement the wayward, conversational manner of the second provides a vivid contrast. The very impressive use of pizzicato in the Adagio, the brilliant string-writing and the feeling of suspense produced by long trills in the Finale are all new and significant features that added to the resources of quartet-writing. And even at its most massive moments, the texture does not suggest that of a compressed orchestral score. Of the three 'Rasumovsky' Quartets it is the longest and gives perhaps the fullest and most comprehensive picture of Beethoven's personality at this stage of his career. Of the contemporary orchestral works, it comes nearest, in its massive power and side range of mood, to the third symphony; the broadly melodious flow of the first movement also has kinship with that of the Violin Concerto.

5

Op 59 (continued)

BEETHOVEN was fond of writing two or more works for the same medium but widely different in mood, and it would be hard to find a stronger contrast than that between the first and second 'Rasumovsky' Quartets. The second is, apart from its slow movement, terser, darker in colour, more highly strung, and less spacious in its material. The opening of the first movement, with its temporary shift to the key a semitone above the tonic, has an obvious kinship with that of the 'Appassionata'. In its original sketch:

Ex 25

it was more abrupt than the final version, though it already had that very distinctive arrangement of the notes of the triad which appears so often in the music of Brahms. But the addition of the two introductory chords followed by a bar of silence and the extension of the two-bar phrases to three bars add immensely to the atmosphere of suspense and mystery that characterise the opening of this work. But it is not as unrelievedly sombre and tense as the first movement of the 'Appassionata'. There is a subsidiary theme of a gently elegiac nature and the second group covers a remarkable variety of mood. Prepared by a very attractive murmuring passage, it begins gracefully and lyrically, but its course is soon roughened by vigorous rhythmic phrases and eventually a strenuous climax is reached after an exciting *crescendo* of syncopated chords. This exposition is as different as possible from the broad and sustained flow of that in the first movement of the F major Quartet. Behind its changing moods there is a powerful nervous energy which, after the repeat of the exposition, seems to explode in the abrupt and dramatic modulation from G to E♭ which leads into the development.

The development begins with a return to the mood and the material of the opening, the atmosphere of suspense being deepened by more dramatic silences and a perpetual shifting of tonality. The two chords appear first in E♭ major, then in E♭ minor, and finally move towards B minor, which is not, after all, a very remote key. It is worth for a moment turning from this passage to two by Mozart, both from the G minor Symphony. At the beginning of the development of the first movement there is an unexpected and striking modulation to F♯ minor, a very remote key in which the music remains for some time. Something rather similar occurs at the equivalent moment in the Finale; there the manner is more aggressive and the mystification more prolonged, but in the end it proves to have led no further afield than the dominant. Both passages are arresting in their context and both lie slightly outside Mozart's normal idiom: the first depends for its effect on the remoteness of the key to which it goes, and the second, not so much on the ends of the journey, as on the process of travel. The same applies to the opening of the development of the first movement of Beethoven's E minor Quartet; it stands out of its context less than either of the Mozart passages, but its sense of mystery is more profound than the passage from the Finale of the G minor Symphony because of its more deliberate manner and more varied dynamics. The first part of this development is very restless tonally; B minor is soon abandoned for more remote keys and a more lyrical version of the main theme in A♭ major very soon gives place to more agitated moods. One of the most striking features is a passage that is rhythmically similar though not identical with the syncopated *crescendo* that occurred towards the end of the exposition. This occurs twice, modulating as it proceeds, and it culminates in an immensely powerful climax based on the opening chords of the movement, which are worked against a vigorous counter-point in semiquavers. Apart from a reappearance of the elegiac subsidiary theme from the first group, the latter part of the development is very energetic; and it ends with a strongly rhythmic passage in octaves. After this an exact recapitulation of the first two bars of the movement would have been an inadequate preparation for the return of the main theme. They are therefore extended to four, with the semiquaver counter-point providing a restless background and filling in the silences.

A first movement in a minor key whose second group is in the relative major gives the composer scope for considerable variety in the recapitulation; Tovey pointed out many years ago that on these occasions Haydn, especially in his late works, would quite often recapitulate the second group in the tonic major, whereas Mozart preferred the tonic minor, with re-markably beautiful results. Beethoven's methods vary con-siderably; sometimes he compromises, beginning in the major and ending in the minor. This is done on an enormous scale in the ninth symphony, and with the utmost conciseness in the Piano Sonata, Op 111. When, as in Op 59, No 2 and the fifth symphony, he recapitulates the whole second group in the major, it will inevitably commit him to writing an extended coda in order to establish the tonality; on the rare occasions when he allows a first movement in a minor key to end in the major, it always happens at the last moment. The codas that have just been mentioned achieve their ends in very different ways. That of the fifth symphony is an immensely powerful peroration in which the explosive energy of the whole movement acquires a new breadth. In the E minor Quartet the coda has greater variety of mood and recalls some of the most striking features of the development. First comes the mysterious passage of suspense with which it began; this leads to a very impressive meditation on the first three notes of the theme, beginning in the remote key of G♯ minor and moving back with a deliberate pace very characteristic of Beethoven. The syncopated *crescendo* that occurred twice in the development is now recalled, but this time there is no modulation, the harmony remaining firmly rooted in a dominant minor ninth on B. The elegiac accessory theme from the first group then appears quietly and works up to a brief climax at which the first theme makes its final bow *fortissimo* and then quietly and unceremoniously disappears. Quite apart from the first four notes of the main theme, the movement as a whole has a decided foretaste of Brahms, especially perhaps the first movement of his Clarinet Quintet. But a comparison between the two movements also reveals characteristic differences. In Brahms there are moments of great power, but the more wistful and nostalgic moods predominate; in Beethoven, on the other hand, the lyrical moments are the more shortlived, and the sense of dramatic suspense far more insistent.

It is curious that all Beethoven's works in E major or minor have all their movements in one or other of these keys. But it is quite clear that for Beethoven the two keys suggested very different moods. In both Piano Sonatas in E major the central movement in E minor provides a strong contrast between the two others and there is the same contrast in the Sonata in E minor, Op 90, between the sombre and passionate first movement and the gently lyrical Rondo in E major that follows it. In the second 'Rasumovsky' Quartet the Adagio in E major, though it would sound infinitely beautiful in any context, is particularly effective after the sombre close of the preceding movement. Like the Adagio of the F major Quartet it is in full sonata form, but with very different results, the one movement, despite its very slow pace, being full of dramatic tension and the other one of the most profoundly serene that Beethoven ever wrote. The broad chorale-like tune with which it opens seems at once to call for the rich and simple block harmony that Beethoven could always use with distinction; in fact he had already written something not unlike it in the quiet central episode of the Finale of the Violin Sonata in A minor, Op 23. But here the entry of the instruments one by one produces a new and strangely ethereal effect and in the fourth bar the move by the second violin from D♯ to D♮ on the fourth beat is strongly prophetic of later works. The tune is harmonised in five different ways during the course of the movement, always with some distinctive feature. After its first presentation it is repeated with the tune played in octaves by the second violin and viola, against a flowing rhythmic counterpoint played by the first violin. This is the first indication of an important feature of the movement, an undercurrent of quietly persistent rhythm, often produced either by dotted notes or triplets, which seems to emphasise rather than disturb its deeply contemplative atmosphere. Its remarkable continuity is due largely to the fact that, although in full sonata form, the usual landmarks and transitions are presented very unobtrusively, which, again, looks ahead to Beethoven's latest period. After the melodious and leisurely bridge passage the second subject enters quietly and with beautiful effect, under a rising scale, to be followed shortly by an exquisite passage marked *mancando*, which is later used in the development.

The exposition passes imperceptibly into the development when the rocking theme of the codetta is interrupted by the first subject appearing in the second violin part, surrounded by rich harmony, and modulating dramatically to D major. But the codetta theme returns and for some time its quietly

C

persistent triplet rhythm dominates the development, rising to a climax in F♯ minor. This, however, soon subsides and after a reference to the *mancando* passage the recapitulation begins very unobtrusively. The main theme is played by the first violin, but it is not allowed a very prominent place, as underneath it the cello recalls the flowing rhythmic counterpoint that was played against it early in the movement, and above it the second violin introduces a new and much broader counter-melody. After this, apart from necessary modifications of key, there are no important changes in the recapitulation until the return of the codetta theme in a less restful and more nostalgic mood than before. This soon leads to the supreme climax of the movement:

Ex 26

in which the first theme makes its final appearance in a high register, over new and striking harmonies, with no competing counter-melodies. This has an overpowering effect similar to that of the final appearance of the first theme of the opening movement of Op 59, No 1, and it is interesting to notice the simplification of the third bar, which had previously appeared

in an early sketch of the tune. The codetta theme then returns
and its quiet triplet movement continues uninterrupted until
the penultimate bar of the movement. The statement that Beethoven was inspired to write this movement by the contemplation of a starlit sky was made independently by Czerny and
the violinist Holz and is considerably less improbable than
many similar stories. Whether or not the story is true, it is
important to remember that a mood of profound and serene
contemplation was, all through Beethoven's life, at least as
characteristic of him as were his more stormy moods. The
'Appassionata' has already been mentioned in connection with
this quartet and in both works there is a strong contrast of
mood between the first two movements. But in the stormy
tragedy of the 'Appassionata' the slow movement, for all its
solemn calm, could not be expected to be more than a passing
relief and it was inevitable that it should be swept violently
aside before its completion. On the other hand the Quartet in
E minor, though powerfully dramatic, is certainly not a
tragedy and it was therefore possible for the profoundly serene
tranquillity of the Adagio to expand at great length without
being at variance with the rest of the quartet.

Among the sketches for this work appears a pleasant little tune:

Ex 27

which was presumably intended for the third movement. But
for various reasons it is easy to see why it was not eventually
used. Apart from the unlikelihood of the two central movements being in the same key, its courtly mood would not have
fitted well with the other movements. But indirectly it played
a part in the C major Quartet: the five-note figure at the beginning of the second bar appears at the end of the exposition

of the first movement; and the fourth bar, with the cadence on the third beat, in addition to the general character of the tune, strongly foreshadows the Minuet of Op 59, No 3. The eventual third movement of the E minor Quartet also has a suggestion of a dance rhythm, but of a far more sombre and agitated kind: Joseph de Marliave, in his erratic but interesting study of the quartets, likened it with some justice to a Chopin mazurka. The main part of the movement is dominated by the distinctive rhythm of its first bar, and the very unusual modulation from E minor to D major at the end of the first section has a curiously restless effect. Like everything in the E minor Quartet, this Allegretto is very unlike the equivalent movement in the first 'Rasumovsky' Quartet; it is simpler in form and, for the most part, more direct in its emotional expression. After a dramatic emphasis of the chord of the Neapolitan sixth, the return of the main theme with a simple but very telling counter-melody in the higher register of the cello is a moment of singular beauty and pathos. In the Trio, described simply as *maggiore*, the second of the two Russian folksongs, originally a solemn hymn, is robbed of its ecclesiastical associations and made to take part in a lively fugue, first against a counter-subject consisting of legato triplets and then against another, of staccato quavers. It is perhaps rather impersonal, except in its final stages, when an exhilaratingly uncompromising canon gradually melts into a gentler mood, leading back beautifully to the *da capo*. After this both the Trio and the main section are played once more, as in the fourth and seventh symphonies and the 'Archduke' Trio.

Gerald Abraham, in his very interesting *Musical Pilgrim* booklet on the middle-period quartets, suggests that it was the prevalence of the tonalities of E minor and major in the first three movements that made Beethoven feel the necessity of starting his Finale out of its key. It is clear from the sketchbooks that he had the idea some time before he finally evolved the main theme of the movement; it is fascinating to see how the sketches gradually get nearer and nearer to the final form of the tune. In the first:

Ex 28

there is nothing in common except for key scheme and a phrase consisting of two quavers and a crotchet. In the next:

Ex 29

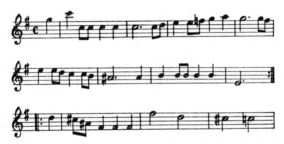

there are features in bars 5 and 9 that occur in the eventual version and in Ex 30 we meet for the first time the opening phrase:

Ex 30

Finally Ex 31 vividly anticipates the theme, not as it appears at the beginning of the movement, but in a different form that comes in the central development; it also contains an important cadential phrase:

Ex 31

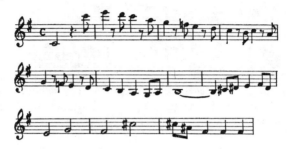

But the quavers that give so delightful and exhilarating a lilt to the theme in its eventual form are still absent. Some twenty years later, in the Finale of the C♯ minor Quartet, Beethoven returned to the same | ♩ ♩ ♩ | rhythm, but there it is more persistent, in a slower tempo and a far more menacing atmosphere.

In the music of the nineteenth century there are several instances of finales that open in a foreign key. In some cases, such as Mendelssohn's String Quartet in E♭ major, Op 12, Schumann's Piano Quintet and Dvořák's Symphony in F major, the foreign key remains undisturbed for some time; in others, such as Beethoven's Quartet in B♭ major, Op 130, and Brahms' String Quintet in G major, the real key is established soon. In Op 59, No 2 the distinctive feature is the hilarious gusto with which Beethoven constantly switches to and fro between the keys of C major and E minor; Schubert, in the Finale of his Piano Sonata in B♭ major, does much the same thing in a more lyrical and less boisterous manner. Beethoven's

Finale is one of his most remarkable, and it rivals that of the eighth symphony in its highly characteristic blend of high spirits and profundity. When the main theme, after numerous wilful attempts to break away to C major, has at last settled in E minor, it is followed by a bridge passage which is built on the first three notes of the theme and also recalls the rhythm of the early sketch given here as Ex 28, thereby showing that this sketch has more in common with the main theme than might appear at a passing glance. The form of the movement is debatable; it could be classified as a sonata form in which the main theme returns before and not after the development, like the first movement of Brahms' Piano Quartet in G minor. But it could also be considered a sonata rondo in which the main theme fails to reappear after the central episode or development, and the theme itself is certainly more characteristic of a rondo than of a movement in sonata form.

The melody of the first episode, in B minor, is surprisingly gentle, but it soon gives place to a long and exhilarating passage in which the first three notes of the theme are tossed from one instrument to another as in the Finale of Op 18, No 3. Inevitably this leads to a return of the theme itself. The central episode is not long, but is full of incident. First the quavers of the main theme run riot in a strenuous contrapuntal passage, after which the theme returns quietly, in a form very similar to the sketch quoted as Ex 31. A fragment of this (bars 6 and 7 of Ex 31) breaks away from its context in a manner highly characteristic of Beethoven and after more vigorous counterpoint, it leads, not to the main theme but, *via* the original bridge passage, to the plaintive melody of the first episode, which is prolonged to twice its original length. The main theme returns, prepared as before, and at this stage the movement might well be drawing towards its close. But, as in the Finale of the eighth symphony, Beethoven still has plenty more to say. When the theme has eventually settled in E minor it is followed by a long coda. It starts with great energy, but this soon gives place to a quiet, nostalgic meditation on the cadential phrase referred to above in connection with Ex 31. The first five notes of the main theme then appear in a menacing mood and rise to a climax. But despite two angry explosions the more pensive mood is not easily pushed aside and there is a very impressive lull with slowly moving chromatic harmonies and for a moment it almost seems as if the movement might be approaching a quiet end. But instead, the main theme makes a last desperate attempt to break away into C major; it is soon, however, forced back into E minor and makes its first appearance in the key of the tonic. Its galloping rhythm continues unbroken almost to the end and there is an odd touch of restlessness before the final close. Of the three finales of Op 59 this is perhaps the most striking and it provides a magnificent climax to one of Beethoven's most powerful works.

The third 'Rasumovsky' Quartet is as different from the other two as they are from each other. It has not quite the sweeping breadth and power of the others and is on the whole less memorable thematically. On the other hand it made the most immediate appeal of the three when first heard, and this, as Abraham has pointed out, may well be due to the fact that it contains features that have roots in the eighteenth century. But side by side with these are others of astonishing originality and the combination of these seemingly contradictory aspects gives the work an attractively wayward character of its own. The introduction to the first movement contrasts strongly with what follows. This in itself was not a new idea; in addition to the famous introduction in Mozart's great C major Quartet there are magnificent instances in several of the later Haydn symphonies. We have already seen how in the Finale of Op 18, No 6 the contrast is too extreme to be stylistically convincing; on the other hand in the first movement of the fourth sym-

phony, written at about the same time as Op 59, it is magical.
In all of these the introduction has some kind of thematic
feature which, had the composer so decided, could have been
developed at greater length. But in the third 'Rasumovsky'
Quartet the introduction is concerned solely with creating an
atmosphere of mystery and suspense, through slowly shifting
chromatic harmonies with no suggestion of either theme or
tonality. It would be hard to find anywhere else in Beethoven's
music a passage that relies so predominantly on colour for its
own sake. It is almost startling to turn from this to the original
sketch of the theme of the first movement:

Ex 32

This has a strong eighteenth-century flavour about it; bars 3
and 4 immediately recall certain passages from Mozart,
especially a theme from the first movement of his Clarinet
Quintet. It would be very interesting to know whether Beethoven, at the time of making this sketch, also had in mind the
introduction; in juxtaposition, the two would have produced
much the same sense of incongruity as in the Finale of Op 18,
No 6. In its final form the theme of the first movement retains
certain melodic features of the sketch but in general character
it is completely transformed; the four-bar phrases are expanded
to five bars, incorporating a terse rhythmic figure of two notes
which dominates the movement. In some ways the music is
curiously capricious; here and there are phrases that look
back to the eighteenth century, while sometimes, as at the odd

progression where Beethoven almost modulates to F major and changes his mind at the last moment:

Ex 33

it looks far ahead.

The key of C major is less common in the music of Beethoven than in that of Haydn and Mozart and their contemporaries. When Beethoven uses it for slow movements it often expresses the deepest serenity as in the Piano Sonata, Op 111. But in quick movements it is usually the key of brilliance, sometimes broad and triumphant, as in the Finale of the fifth symphony, sometimes tempered by mysterious shadows, as in the first movement of the 'Waldstein' Sonata. The first and last movements of Op 59, No 3 are also characterised by brilliance, in the latter more dynamic and powerful, in the former more subtle and whimsical. In the exposition both the first and second groups are built on lively rhythmic phrases rather than sustained lyrical melodies. The cadential trill near the end of the second group is a feature that had by this time become slightly archaic, but it appears at a similar moment in the first movement of the 'Waldstein' Sonata and, with a wonderful and mysterious difference, in the Violin Concerto. Abraham draws some interesting parallels between this movement and that of Mozart's C major Quartet, K. 465, but the brittle texture and semi-jocular manner of Beethoven's movement come nearer in spirit to Haydn than to Mozart; Haydnesque also is the very imaginative treatment of the all-important rhythmic figure of the first subject (compare Exs 33 and 34):

Ex 34

The incisive phrases of the first subject are followed by a lively bridge passage, and the second group brings no marked change of mood, though there is a brief but impressive lull at one point. The development section is the most imaginative part of the movement. Mention has already been made of the Piano Sonata in B♭ major, Op 22, in connection with the Op 18 quartets; its first movement also has points in common with that of Op 59, No 3. In both movements there comes a moment, towards the end of the development, when the generally clear-cut and incisive character of the music gives place temporarily to something much broader and more mysterious. The development of the sonata movement is dominated by the last phrase of the exposition, which gradually loses its aggressive character and appears in a much smoother and quieter version, against a background of rustling semiquavers and slowly moving harmonies. In the C major Quartet the development, though not long, is more eventful. All the different elements of the first group are referred to, in the same order in which they appeared in the exposition, ending with Ex 34. Then the ubiquitous two-note figure detaches itself from its context and expands into an extraordinary passage, persistent in rhythm and deliberate in its harmonic movement:

Ex 35

This moves very impressively for a few bars into Db major, a key which to Beethoven usually suggested a mood of mysterious solemnity, and returns gradually for the recapitulation, which begins very unobtrusively with a varied version of the main theme. The passage from the Bb major Piano Sonata is an early and very successful example of the peculiar feeling of suspense that was one of Beethoven's most significant contributions to the development of music. But in the C major Quartet it is done with a boldness and power that show how immeasurably Beethoven's style had developed between 1800 and 1806. Once started, the recapitulation runs a regular course and the coda, though very effective, is unusually short for a work of this period.

It appears from the sketch-books that the first idea for the slow movement of this quartet was the theme eventually used for the Allegretto of the seventh symphony. The tune that eventually supplanted it, also in the key of A minor, is of peculiarly haunting quality, and the whole movement exceptionally original. It makes no attempt to emulate the massive solemnity of the slow movements of the F major and E minor Quartets and its gently elegiac mood foreshadows certain movements of Mendelssohn, though far surpassing him in rhythmic variety and flexibility. It was suggested by Marion Scott that, though not so labelled by Beethoven, the main theme of the movement was a Russian folk-tune, but it is not so much the melody itself as the pedal points and persistent pizzicato notes over which it is presented that suggest a Slavonic atmosphere. This is especially true of the haunting refrain that appears after the first theme has run its course. The form of the movement is hard to classify. A bridge passage built on a strangely melancholy phrase introduced by the viola leads to a more animated second theme in the relative major, which is in due course followed by a kind of development, built mainly on the bridge passage. All this suggests a movement in sonata form, but the development is followed by a return, not of the first theme but of the second subject, first in A major and then, after a striking modulation, in the remote key of E♭ major, where it culminates in a flowing passage of semiquavers which Mendelssohn almost reproduced at the end of the slow movement of his Violin Concerto. The return of the main theme is brought about in a very impressive and characteristic manner, with slowly moving harmonies over a persistent stream of pizzicato quavers. The final section of the movement consists of the main theme, with the original repeats written out in varied form, some very effective new scoring, and a coda based on the refrain mentioned before and reminiscences of the development; the mysterious pizzicato quavers have the last word. The tone-colour of the movement is highly individual and the pizzicato notes played by the cello, varying both in length and in loudness, have an almost hypnotic effect. In several movements from early Haydn quartets written at a time when the distinction between orchestral and chamber music was still imperfectly defined, a simple pizzicato accompaniment was continued without a break, as in the well-known Serenade from Op 3, No 5. But in the later chamber works, both of Haydn and of Mozart, pizzicato is used far more sparingly. In the Trio of the Minuet of his Quartet in D minor Mozart uses it to provide a picturesque contrast to the powerfully contrapuntal texture of the Minuet, but in the slow introduction to the Finale of the String Quintet in G minor the pizzicato notes played by the cello produce an effect of great solemnity. In Beethoven's earlier chamber works there is some attractive use of pizzicato, more in the string trios than in the quartets, but it was in the slow movements of Op 59, Nos 1 and 3 that he first realised to the full its emotional possibilities.

The introduction and the second movement are undoubtedly the most original parts of the C major Quartet. In different ways and on different scales they are both remarkable pieces of sustained mood-painting, relying on half-shades and entirely free from rhetorical gestures. They also provide a striking contrast to the brilliance of the quick movements, the Minuet coming somewhere between the two extremes. This has a demure exterior which led Vincent d'Indy to dismiss it, summarily and unjustifiably, as 'a return to the style of 1796'. Although it is the most simply constructed movement of the work, it evidently gave Beethoven some trouble. The tune quoted as Ex 27 may well have been the original germ; already it has the cadence on the third beat of the bar which is a marked feature of the final version and not characteristic of the eighteenth-century minuet. There is another, longer sketch in which the Minuet is in F and the Trio in D♭. The melody of the Minuet is still some distance from its ultimate form, though the rhythm of the first bar is present. Two more sketches appear, far nearer to the final version, but it is only in the last of these that the Minuet and Trio are in their eventual keys of C and F respectively. The texture of the Minuet, especially after the return of the theme in the bass, is beautifully wrought and the Trio shows well the vitality and individuality with which Beethoven could use ideas that were built basically on scales and arpeggios. But the most imaginative part of the movement is the coda, which casts a mysterious shadow over the first phrase of the Minuet, taking it through

C minor and E♭, to wait on the dominant seventh of C for the opening of the Finale.

Inspired perhaps by the last movement of Haydn's Op 64, No 5, Beethoven was often attracted by the idea of a *moto perpetuo* Finale, the earliest instance being the very lively Presto with which the String Trio in G major ends. The later examples vary greatly in mood and it is clear that for Beethoven the idea of perpetual motion did not necessarily imply a breakneck pace. The finales of the 'Appassionata' Sonata and the fourth symphony, which illustrate well Beethoven's fondness for doing the same kind of thing more than once, but with widely different results, are both marked 'Allegro ma non troppo' and lose much if taken too fast. Similarly the last movements of the Piano Sonatas in D minor and F major, Op 54, the one lyrical and the other gently argumentative, both go at a leisurely Allegretto pace. But the latter of these, with its persistent semiquaver movement and quasi-contrapuntal texture, is in some ways a forerunner of what Beethoven did in a far more dynamic manner in the Finale of Op 59, No 3. Here, for the first time since the G major String Trio, the motion is not only perpetual but precipitate and Beethoven faces the interesting problem of combining sonata form with fugal texture. Mozart's solutions of this are fascinatingly dissimilar. In the Finale of the String Quartet in G major, K. 387, he stresses, with obvious relish, the contrast between contrapuntal and non-contrapuntal; the result is a delightful and entertaining patchwork, of a kind that could only have succeeded in the hands of a composer possessed of a very light touch and a strong sense of proportion. In the overture to *The Magic Flute*, on the other hand, the fugal element is more predominant, though not exclusively so; the movement is practically monothematic, the main theme being of a kind that can fit with equal ease into any kind of texture.

The Finale of the third 'Rasumovsky' Quartet comes, in its

methods, somewhere between the two Mozart movements and
is nearer to the *Magic Flute* overture. But its whole course is
affected by the nature of its theme, which is so long and
straggling that there is only room for two complete sets of
entries, one at the beginning and the other at the start of the
recapitulation. The rapid quaver movement hardly ever ceases;
sometimes it is combined, in a manner very characteristic of
Beethoven, with slowly moving harmony, as in the powerful
and non-contrapuntal bridge passage. One of the most important features of the movement is the little figure of four
notes on which the last two bars of the theme are built; it
forms the basis of much of the development and of the long
and elaborately prepared climax. The playfully imitative
second subject does not contribute much towards the general
scheme of the movement; the development is based mainly
on fragments of the subject treated with much energy and
resource and there are also references to the vigorous bridge
passage. Over and above all this is the immense spaciousness
of the whole design and the power of the modulations; especially characteristic is the fiercely indignant passage in C♯ minor.
After a pause the recapitulation begins with a fugal exposition
of the complete subject, this time accompanied by a new
counter-theme in steadily tramping minims. After it has run
its course it is followed by a highly eventful and dramatic coda.
Some reminiscences of the early part of the development lead
to a remarkable passage in which a fragment of the main theme
is repeated persistently against the counter-subject in minims
and a series of long trills. Then the first violin plays a long
stream of uninterrupted quavers against very deliberately
moving harmonies and this leads to what appears to be the
final climax. But at the last moment it is held up by two
dramatic pauses. Much of the previous passage is repeated with
modifications, and at last the end comes with an air of immense finality. The fugal element plays an important part in

the movement, but it is the powerful rhythmic drive and the broad harmonic outline behind the counterpoint that gives the music its peculiar exhilaration. Here Beethoven has not time for the contrapuntal elaborations of the Finale of Mozart's 'Jupiter' Symphony or of his own later fugues; he is concerned mainly with over-all effects and the result, judged on its own merits, is irresistible.

6

Op 74 and 95

THE three works that comprise Op 59 are the most exuberant and richly scored of Beethoven's quartets; the next two move gradually in the direction of the sparer texture and more withdrawn manner of the last works. The Quartet in E♭ major, Op 74, is full and mellow in sound, but for the most part more intimate and thoughtful than any of the 'Rasumovsky' Quartets. Its first movement, like that of the C major Quartet, has a slow introduction in which the tonality is ambiguous but not so completely obscured as in the earlier work. It fluctuates between E♭ and A♭ until the last seven bars; these bring a cloud of chromaticism from which the opening bars of the Allegro emerge dramatically. In this introduction Beethoven depends less predominantly on harmonic colour than in that of the C major Quartet, and the dotted-note rhythm of the last bars foreshadows, perhaps subconsciously, a feature of the first theme of the Allegro. About twenty years later Mendelssohn, in his String Quartet in E♭ major, Op 12, wrote a slow introduction in many ways very similar to that of Beethoven's Op 74; but, though most agreeable, it lacks the peculiar atmosphere of mystery and romance that is so characteristic of Beethoven's passage.

The Allegro is remarkable, not so much for any individual thematic feature as for its continuity of structure and warmth of colour. The exposition is very concise; the first group is not,

as so often in Beethoven's music, dominated by a single phrase
but consists of two contrasted ideas:

Ex 36

Ex 37

These are followed by a very original bridge passage in which
the first two notes of Ex 36, played pizzicato, are tossed from
one instrument to another against a background of repeated
chords; it is for this, and its subsequent developments, that the
work has been nicknamed the 'Harp Quartet'. The second
group contains some lively imitative writing, some striking
patches of harmonic colour and a very characteristic cadential
phrase, but no marked contrast of mood. The development
opens with a modulation from B♭ major to G major, which in
an early sketch was done gradually, but in the final version far
more directly and abruptly. The expansion of Ex 37 that
follows is of remarkable power and energy. The first two bars
are treated imitatively; then the whole phrase appears with
great sonority in C major, to be followed by a rousing continuation based on the dotted-note rhythm of the fourth and
fifth bars. Very deliberately the music moves from C major to
the dominant of E♭ major and there is a long passage of
suspense built on the pizzicato notes of the bridge passage,
which are expanded into arpeggios of increasing rapidity. The
slow harmonic movement in the latter part of the development
has a particularly striking effect after the very terse exposition
and Beethoven's unflagging energy prevents the music from

stagnating in any way. After the recapitulation, in which there are some interesting digressions in the bridge passage, the coda matches the development in spaciousness. It begins with an impressive lull, in which the chord of the diminished seventh is used, as in the introduction of the C major Quartet, not sentimentally or rhetorically, but to convey a sense of mystery and uncertainty. After a crescendo in which the second bar of Ex 37 is treated imitatively, the first violin provides a brilliant and sonorous background, first to the pizzicato arpeggios and then to the phrase from Ex 37, culminating in a carefully prepared and very emphatic cadence. In all this passage Beethoven achieves a truly symphonic breadth and spaciousness without any sense of strain on the medium. The cadential phrase with which the exposition ended appears once more and the final bars of the movement remind us that the pizzicato arpeggios were derived from Ex 36.

This very original and subtly constructed piece of music is followed by one of the most directly appealing movements that Beethoven ever wrote. It has affinities, as Marion Scott pointed out, with the Adagio, also in A♭ major, of the 'Pathetic' Sonata and it is in the same simple rondo form, though much more complex in detail. The long main melody seems to have come into existence with more spontaneity than many of Beethoven's tunes and the different colouring of its three appearances is one of the chief charms of the movement. At first it suggests a mood of Olympian serenity, with the first violin playing high above the other instruments. The second time the atmosphere is more restless, with the melody varied and begun an octave lower and more movement in the other parts; at its third appearance the tune begins an octave lower still, on middle C, and gradually works its way upwards through a maze of picturesque accompanying figures. The two episodes are equally melodious, but are contrasted in general character. The first, which is the longer and more eventful, starts in A♭ minor and goes through various nearly related keys. Towards the end of the episode it becomes obvious that the return of the main theme cannot be far away, but Beethoven quietly prolongs the suspense in a highly characteristic way, with passing glances in unexpected directions. The melody of the second episode is so spacious and attractive that it might well have been allowed to play a more important part; the moment when the cello steps in and quietly takes the stage is of exquisite beauty:

Ex 38

equally so are the echoing phrases played against it by the first violin. The tune modulates from D♭ to A♭, the home tonic, a key in which it would be impossible to stay at such a moment; Beethoven therefore introduces a very impressive reminiscence of the first theme in A♭ minor. Even from here too quick a return would be ineffective and as at the end of the first episode, the suspense is prolonged, this time rather more dramatically, with a surprisingly menacing reference to the main theme. The coda looks back first to the melody of the first episode and then to various portions of the main theme; the very deliberate and leisurely close is eminently suited to the general character of the movement.

The third movement of Op 74 contrasts strongly with the rest of the work. The familiar ♪♪♪♩ rhythm that occurs in so many of Beethoven's works of this period appears here at a more precipitate pace than elsewhere; at the same time the broad energy, as so often, is guided by a firm and broad harmonic outline. It is in the same design as the third movements of Op 59, No 2 and the fourth and seventh symphonies, consisting of Scherzo, Trio, Scherzo, Trio, Scherzo. With all its power and vehemence, the movement has an odd, enigmatic quality which it shares with the Scherzo of the fifth symphony. It opens with great vigour which soon explodes in a tremendously exciting outburst in D♭. But after this, until the end of the main scherzo section, the music becomes gradually more and more subdued and mysterious; one of the most impressive moments is when a haunting fragment of tune is played over the persistent rhythm that dominates the movement:

Ex 39

The atmosphere of this is shattered abruptly by the harshly aggressive mood of the Trio, a mood which in Beethoven frequently goes with a fugal texture. Here again there is an affinity with the corresponding section of the fifth symphony, but in the Quartet the texture is barer and the colour more glaring. The pace is increased from 'Presto' to 'Più presto quasi prestissimo' and the main subject, which has a surprising melodic resemblance to that of the Andante of Op 59, No 3, rushes along in unbroken crotchets, with a strong accent on the first beat of every other bar. The other parts move entirely in dotted minims, sometimes tied so as to produce suspensions. Here there is no lessening of energy, as in the Trio of the fifth symphony, but a defiant diminished seventh leads to the *da*

capo. When, after the second appearance of the Trio, the Scherzo appears for the last time, the dynamics, after the first eight bars, are drastically reduced, and the music moves quietly and with great deliberation from C minor through D♭ major to the dominant of E♭ major, leading without a break into the Finale.

This process suggests again a comparison with the transition from Scherzo to Finale in the slightly earlier fifth symphony, in which subdued and sinister twilight gradually brightens into a triumphant exultation. In the quartet the sequence is reversed, the hammering energy of the Scherzo slowly subsiding into tranquillity. This is probably the harder to achieve convincingly without a sense of anticlimax; it was very characteristic of Beethoven to write these two very dissimilar passages within a few years of each other and not surprising that the long *crescendo* in the fifth symphony was the earlier of the two. The Finale of Op 74 is a set of variations, a form not very often used by Beethoven for last movements. The most outstandingly great instances are the magnificent slow finales of the Piano Sonatas, Op 109 and 111. Those of the third and ninth symphonies, though they both contain elements of variation, are difficult to put into any category; the three remaining instances, from this quartet and the Violin Sonatas, Op 30, No 1 and Op 96, aim mainly at lyrical repose and are all marked 'Allegretto'. The theme of this set consists mainly of short phrases that begin both harmonically and melodically halfway through the bar, which gives it a curiously hesitant character. The tonal scheme, with its pull towards the mediant, is also unusual and may have influenced Brahms in the theme of the variations in his String Quartet in B♭ major.

The first five variations keep quite closely to the general outline of the theme, but differ considerably from each other in texture. In the first the vigorous staccato counterpoint cuts neatly across the rhythmic landmarks of the theme. To this the second variation provides a charming lyrical contrast with a

flowing melody in almost unbroken quaver triplets played by
the viola against a harmonic background that is at first very
simple but becomes slightly more elaborate in the second half.
Although there is no change of pace in these five variations
there is a marked contrast of mood between numbers one,
three and five, which are lively and energetic, and two and
four, which are more thoughtful. In the first half of the third,
the second violin and cello run about vigorously in tenths for
most of the time; in the fourth the first violin plays the tune,
not in an elaborated but in simplified form, over a texture of
great beauty; the pull towards the mediant is intensified at the
end of the first half and proportionately lessened at the beginning of the second. The rather prosaically energetic fifth
variation, less interesting in itself, enhances the extraordinary
change of atmosphere caused by the opening of the sixth. The
pace is slightly quickened but the tonic pedal note in triplets
that continues throughout the first half gives a sense of increased spaciousness. Not only is the music prevented from
going towards the mediant, but is pulled quietly but firmly in
the opposite direction when, at the beginning of the second
half, the pedal note moves from Eb to Db. Before the end of
the variation it returns as unceremoniously as it went, but
obviously a considerable amount of coda is needed before a
feeling of finality can be established. The melody of the first
four bars of this last variation is played several times against a
dominant pedal note, still in triplets. Soon there is an emphatic
cadence but even after this a curious harmonic progression:

Ex 40

which suggests a kind of tonal uncertainty. This, however, is quelled in a brisk and business-like way by an increasingly animated set of three variations on a drastically truncated version of the theme. The first is in a lively dactylic rhythm, the second in triplets and the third recalls the semiquavers of the original third variation, played this time in octaves. Finally the quartet ends with two quiet, detached chords.

Looking back for a moment at the work as a whole, we see that it presents in some ways a less vividly marked personality than the 'Rasumovsky' Quartets. Perhaps for this reason different musicians have reacted to it in different ways. The Adagio, for instance, is described by Ernest Walker as 'of the happy rather than the poignant type' while to Daniel Gregory Mason it is 'unrelieved in its sadness'. Similarly Marion Scott has said of the whole work that 'in its outward panoply of music there is a little more of the glory of this world than of the glory of the spirit', while to me it has always seemed to be generally thoughtful, though not ascetic. In any case it is intensely characteristic of Beethoven, especially perhaps in its combination of warmth and richness of sound on the one hand and on the other a feeling that still more could have been said, had the composer so wished.

This sense of reserve is still more pronounced in the next Quartet, Op 95, in F minor, where it is allied to a remarkable power and concentration. Written in 1810 and dedicated to Nicolas Zmeskall von Domanovetz, the work is described on the manuscript as 'Quartett serioso', and the same adjective appears as a direction over the third movement. In general character it is as different as possible from Op 74, being much sparer in texture and, in its first movement, much more explosive in manner. The temporary shift from F minor to G♭ major in the opening bars is reminiscent of the 'Appassionata' Sonata and the second 'Rasumovsky' Quartet, but is done here with far more abruptness. The whole movement is

of great individuality. As a rule the most compressed of his
first movements are emotionally of a piece; either lyrical, as in
the Piano Sonatas in F♯ major, Op 78, and A major, Op 101,
or stormy as in Op 111. Likewise those in which there is most
dramatic contrast of mood, as in the ninth symphony or the
'Appassionata' Sonata, are on a large scale. But in Op 95, in the
words of Tovey, he 'contrives to pack a large symphonic tragedy
into five minutes'. The emotional range is shown in the first ten
bars; the temporary modulation to G♭ mentioned above is not
just a mysterious echo, as in Op 59, No 2 and the 'Appassionata',
but brings with it a suggestion of the tenderness that is a feature
of the movement, though it is frequently brushed aside. The
brusque announcement of the opening theme in octaves:

Ex 41

is very characteristic of Beethoven at any period of his life:
equally so is the way in which the first five notes often detach
themselves from the rest. The choice of the submediant key for
the second group is unusual in Beethoven's works; in the
String Trio in C minor he had used it as a halfway house
between the tonic and the relative major and it is used with
magnificent effect in several later works. In the first movement
of Op 95 the first six bars of the second group are a beautiful
instance of the amount of melodic and rhythmic interest that
Beethoven could infuse into a passage of simple tonic and
dominant harmony. The gently rocking rhythm soon quickens
into a stormy passage based on the first five notes of the main
theme and culminating in a gruff and unexpected scale in a
very remote key. It is followed by some quiet cadential phrases
of great beauty, though the scale reappears for a moment, and
the exposition ends peacefully in D♭ major.

The development breaks in dramatically upon this with a sudden chord of F major; it is very short and built entirely on various elements of the first group, especially the first five notes. One of its most striking features is a mysteriously murmuring figure derived from the leaping octaves of the third and fourth bars of the movement. Unusual also is the fact that it remains all the time in the neighbourhood of the tonic; perhaps for this reason the recapitulation of the first group is severely curtailed. The second group, very surprisingly, appears again in Db major, but after a few bars it moves quietly to F major, and the rest of it is recapitulated regularly except that the aggressive scales come in less remote keys. The coda, like the development, begins dramatically with an interrupted cadence and continues for some time in much the same vein, with indignantly tramping staccato quavers played by the first violin and cello against long notes. The first five notes of the main theme become increasingly persistent and are repeated many times by the viola; finally, after a sudden *diminuendo*, the whole phrase is played twice and the movement ends quietly. This work has often been described as a link between the middle- and late-period quartets, and the abrupt manner of the first movement in particular comes very near to that of certain movements in the posthumous works. At the same time the gestures are more explosive and there is still some of the highly strung rhetoric of the 'Appassionata' Sonata and the E minor Quartet.

In both Op 95 and the 'Appassionata' the juxtaposition of the quiet F minor close of the first movement and the opening of the second is very impressive. In the sonata the choice of key for the slow movement is common enough in itself, but after the large and widely spaced expanse of F minor the rich sound of the darkly coloured chord of Db major gives an effect of great solemnity. In the quartet the change is less rich but stranger. The first movement ends with a bare octave F, and the second begins with the first six notes of the descending scale of D major, played by the cello unaccompanied. The first note bridges the gap between the two very remote keys, suggesting a complete change of scenery the mystery of which is enhanced by the quiet way in which it is accomplished. The second movement, like that of the seventh symphony, has the direction 'Allegretto'; of the three slow movements in Op 59 the third is the one to which it is most akin, but it is more subtle in texture and more deeply thoughtful in tone. The four introductory bars played by the cello are followed by the main theme, which is of extraordinary beauty and sensitiveness. It has a gentle and continuous flow, with a strange undercurrent of restlessness; in the first four bars there is a temporary pull towards G minor and in its later stages this is subtly recalled by frequently recurring B♭'s, sometimes in the melody, but more often in an inner part:

Ex 42

The very delicate chromatic colour is a common characteristic of Beethoven's later work (compare the first two variations in the Finale of Op 111), but here it plays an unusually prominent part. After the extreme terseness of the opening Allegro the leisurely expansiveness of the second movement is particularly impressive. It is in *ABA* form with coda, everything being planned on a spacious scale. When the first theme has run its course, it ends in a surprisingly formal manner with several cadences, the penultimate chord containing the flattened sixth characteristic of the whole movement. The central section opens with a fugal exposition, and here again the subject has a strong pull towards G minor; it was pointed out by Mason that Beethoven could, if so inclined, have combined it with the main theme. The tonality of the central section has a strangely floating, dreamlike quality, resulting from the chromaticism of the subject. After the exposition the entries succeed each other more frequently until the course of the music is interrupted by a mysterious passage based on the descending scale from the introductory bars of the movement. When the fugal texture is resumed the feeling of restlessness is increased by stretti and by the curious fluttering phrases in staccato semiquavers; the subject is inverted and presently its first two notes, inverted and otherwise, are detached from the rest and lead back with deliberation to the return of the first section. This, when at last it comes, has a particularly reposeful effect owing to the fact that the bass has already been on D for several bars before the tonic harmony is heard. The main theme is more ethereally scored, with the melody for the most part an octave higher, and it leads to a long and eventful coda. A stretto on the fugue subject in which all four instruments take part for a moment obscures the tonality, but this is quickly restored by Ex 42, which is expanded into a passage of great breadth culminating in a beautifully prepared high note for the first violin. Shortly after this the movement appears to be on the point of ending quietly, though still with wistful chromatic touches. But after the last cadence comes a bare octave D followed by a diminished seventh, and the next movement follows without a break.

Beethoven had done this before, with the utmost violence, in the 'Appassionata'; here the effect, though gruff and startling, is less catastrophic. The third movement, oddly described as 'Allegro vivace assai, ma serioso', is not a wild and headlong tragedy like the Finale of the 'Appassionata'. It is grim and sardonic in temper but in its persistent rhythm there is the suggestion of a dance, much more aggressive than the Allegretto from Op 59, No 2, but perhaps nearer still to the Mazurka. The first sixteen bars consist of short abrupt phrases which eventually cohere into a more continuous tune. It is not till then that the key of F minor is firmly established, and once fixed it remains unbroken to the end of the section, asserting itself with great vigour in the last four bars. The Trio provides a striking contrast. There is a perpetual flow of smooth quavers, which alternately serve as an accompaniment to the very beautiful main theme:

Ex 43

and form themselves into shapely interludes. The sequence of keys is attractively fluid, the music moving quietly from G♭ major to D major, the key of the previous movement, and from there to B minor and back *via* a diminished seventh to a repeat of the main section. After this the same chord forms the basis of a curiously planned modulation to D major, in which

key the Trio returns in a shortened form, with a different key-
sequence. Soon it works round to C major, from which it is
an easy step to the final return of the main section, this time
beginning at its seventeenth bar and at a quicker pace. The
whole movement, with its alternating fierceness and tenderness, is a fitting counterpart to the opening Allegro; the contrasts in it are however expressed more directly, as is natural
in a movement cast in so sectional a form. Perhaps its most
prophetic feature is to be found in the Trio, where Beethoven
goes in the quietest and most unconcerned way through
modulations that in earlier works would have been carried out
with far more tension. Another forward-looking feature of
both this and the first movement is the unceremoniousness of
the end. Elaborate perorations such as are found at the ends
of the third 'Rasumovsky' Quartet and the fifth and eighth
symphonies become increasingly rare in Beethoven's later
works; even after the prolonged D major jubilations at the
end of the ninth symphony the final silence somehow has the
effect of a shock. And in a work as terse as Op 95 the abrupt
conclusions of the movements are particularly appropriate.

The short introduction to the Finale is a feature that appears
several times in Beethoven's music with very varied results.
The most striking instance among the early works is the
'Malinconia' section in Op 18, No 6, where, as we have seen,
he explores what were then strange and mysterious harmonic
regions so successfully that it was difficult for him to return to
a more humdrum atmosphere without a sense of anticlimax.
Many years later, in the introduction to the Finale of the
Op 106 Sonata, he produces a similar effect of mystification,
but here there is no exploration of the unknown; the impression is rather that of a strange dream in the course of which
echoes of an earlier age float by and disappear. Totally different
from either of these is the Andante un poco Adagio that precedes the Finale of the Quartet in C♯ minor; here there is no

feeling of suspense or mystery, but a stream of slow quiet music of such beauty that one wishes Beethoven had allowed it to develop into a complete movement. The short Larghetto espressivo in Op 95 comes somewhere between these extremes; it has an appealing pathos but its short, questioning phrases do not suggest a possible opening of a complete movement, but seem rather to be constantly expecting something to happen. Its last bars, without any thematic reference, anticipate the repetition of short phrases which is so marked a feature of the main theme of the Finale.

This quartet is known to have been a special favourite of Mendelssohn, and its Finale, Allegretto agitato in 6/8, has a decided foretaste of his music. But the phrases are shorter, tenser and less smoothly rounded and the agitation more apt to burst into flame. The general mood is not unlike that of the first movement of the second 'Rasumovsky' Quartet, but the colouring is less dark and the proportions less expansive. Beethoven's handling of the rondo form is always highly organised and sometimes, as in the Violin Concerto and the 'Waldstein' Sonata, it is developed on a vast and leisurely scale. In the Finale of Op 95 the proportions are the natural outcome of the themes themselves, which all have a restless air that is very far removed from the lyricism of Beethoven's gentler rondos, such as the second movement of the Piano Sonata in E minor, Op 90. Beethoven's handling of them might be described as 'unresting, unhasting'; there is never a moment wasted, but they are never cramped or stunted and he is able to allow himself moments of relaxation. The most striking of these occurs when the main theme has returned for the last time and the main business of the movement is over; it is a deeply impressive meditation built round two fragments of the theme. The harmonic movement is very deliberate, leading eventually to a very soft chord of F major. The movement could almost have ended here, but Beethoven decided otherwise and concluded the work with a light and brilliant coda, the effect of which is very surprising but highly exhilarating. Opinions about it have varied; d'Indy condemned it severely and Mason was worried by it but made a valiant attempt to defend it by endeavouring to connect it thematically with what came before it. Some writers have likened it to the triumphant coda of the 'Egmont' Overture, but it is far gayer and more light-handed, and is best understood if we bear in mind that there was in Beethoven a streak of waywardness which delighted in unexpected changes of mood and became increasingly apparent in his later works. Perhaps the best comment is that of Randall Thompson, quoted by Mason: 'No bottle of champagne was ever uncorked at a better time.'

A brief backward glance at the five quartets of Beethoven's middle period shows at the same time a great variety and a logical and consistent development of style. They all come within a period of five years, but during that comparatively short space of time he could range from the glowing sonority of the first 'Rasumovsky' Quartet to the spare texture and abrupt manner of Op 95. Fourteen years elapsed between Op 95 and Op 127, but in certain ways the F minor Quartet is strongly prophetic of the later quartets; and they, in their turn, with all their new features, could never be described as making a complete break with the past. Between 1810 and 1824 there was no fundamental change of idiom in Beethoven's music. What was perpetually changing, however, was his approach to the problems of composition. To audiences who were accustomed to the more standardised methods of Mozart and even, to a lesser extent, Haydn, this must have been thoroughly bewildering; you could never know where you were with Beethoven. The first movements of the last five piano sonatas, for instance, are all in sonata form, but widely different from each other in every way. It is not merely a question of size; two of the shortest are those of Op 101 and Op 110, of which

D

one is so continuous that it is hard to decide where the first group ends and the second begins, and the other contains a number of themes which follow each other with the clarity and precision of a Mozart sonata. And with the increasing variety of technique came a corresponding increase of emotional range; this culminates in the C♯ minor Quartet, Op 131, which contains music of the deepest thoughtfulness and of an almost light-headed gaiety.

7

Op 127

THE three quartets, Op 127, 132 and 130, were commissioned by Prince Nicholas Galitzin, to whom they were dedicated. As in Op 59, the work in the minor key comes second, and the third, as originally conceived, ended with a fugal movement. The second and third both show unusual features in their design which look ahead to the still more unconventional plan of Op 131; while the first is in the traditional four movements and is full of lyrical beauty of the gentlest and most approachable kind. The key of E♭ major here suggests, not so much the strenuous, heroic moods of the third symphony and the fifth piano concerto, as the mellow warmth of the Trio, Op 70, No 2, the Quartet Op 74 and the Piano Sonata, Op 81, with an added depth and subtlety. The brief Maestoso introduction with which the first movement opens is very different from those in Op 59, No 3 and Op 74. In both of these there is an element of mystery and uncertainty: in Op 127 the key is asserted with the utmost clarity, in a broad and dignified rhythm and magnificently rich harmony. The contrast between this and the flowing lyrical movement that follows suggests the first movement of Mozart's symphony in the same key, K. 543. But there Mozart's style is at its most leisurely; the ideas in the introduction unfold themselves with great deliberation, with a marvellous sense of space in the final bars. Beethoven himself may well have come under the influence of this in the first movement of the seventh symphony; in that of Op 127 the introduction, despite the grandly confident tone of its opening, seems to end with a question to which the main theme of the Allegro supplies the only possible answer, and its two reappearances provide the main element of contrast in a movement of remarkable continuity. A few years earlier, in the Piano Sonata in E major, Op 109, Beethoven had written one of the strangest of his first movements, in which the second subject, in a far slower tempo than the first, seems to comment mysteriously on, without seriously interrupting, the almost unbroken flow of semiquavers that permeate the rest of the movement. In Op 127 the contrasts are less rhapsodical in effect and the texture more highly organised.

The join between the introduction and the Allegro, with its emphasis on the subdominant harmony, looks back to the Piano Sonata in E♭ major, Op 81, but here it takes place far more smoothly. The first theme, with its gently persistent repetitions, might be expected to come from a minuet rather than a movement in sonata form, but it is treated with a resourcefulness and variety of texture that prevent the slightest danger of monotony. It is followed by an equally melodious continuation, and a short imitative passage leads to the second subject. This is as flowing as the first, but more long-breathed in its phrases, and in an unusual key; Beethoven had already used the mediant major, in the Piano Sonatas, Op 31, No 1 and Op 53, but this is the only occasion on which he used the mediant minor. The whole of the exposition has great charm and spontaneity and the reminiscences, near the end, of the first theme are exquisitely done. After the even flow of the exposition, the return of the introduction, in G major, is very dramatic in effect. The sudden *fortissimo* is very characteristic of Beethoven, and the colour is brighter and the chord more widely spaced than at the beginning of the movement. The development is concerned mainly with the first subject

It begins placidly but the texture is broken up more and more, with moments of bareness, e.g.:

Ex 44

that are increasingly common in the last quartets. Soon, however, it becomes extremely full and leads eventually to another return of the introduction. This time it comes, not as a sudden shock, but as the culmination of a powerful *fortissimo* passage and full advantage is taken of the rich sonority of C major. On its last appearance the introduction is reduced from six bars to four; the tempo of the Allegro is resumed and the development continues the treatment of the first theme, which becomes more fragmentary as the music gradually moves towards the tonic. Two little phrases derived from the first and third bars of the theme are repeated with a curious almost hypnotic insistence, until the recapitulation, as in the first movement of the Piano Sonata, Op 101, begins so casually that at first one is hardly aware of what has happened. It follows the traditional plan, but with new details; the first subject appears with a wealth of fresh contrapuntal decorations, the bridge passage is extended and the second subject is not, as might be expected, in the tonic minor, but in the major. The coda, like the latter part of the development, is built upon the first and third bars of the theme, but is entirely different in atmosphere; here Beethoven does not argue over the phrases, but dwells on them quietly and affectionately, often against a simple counterpoint of dotted minims derived from the original bass of the theme. It is very leisurely, but the actual end comes in a gently informal way that leaves us wishing for more.

Beethoven had always been interested in the variation form and, characteristically, he had always tended to approach it from widely different standpoints. In the set for piano in F major, Op 34, for instance, he aims at getting the maximum of variety by contrasts not only of pace but also of key. On the other hand, in the 33 Variations in C minor the contrasts are more smoothly graded, resulting in a highly continuous structure similar to that of Bach's D minor Chaconne for solo violin. The finales of the Piano Sonatas, Op 109 and Op 111, differ from each other in much the same way; in the former the tempo changes several times and in the latter there is an unbroken continuity. The slow movement of Op 127 comes somewhere between these two, but is on the whole nearer to the Arietta from Op 111. The theme appears to have given Beethoven endless trouble; there are innumerable sketches, including a number that are in a different key and tempo, which may have been intended for variations rather than for the theme. The following is one of the most complete:

Ex 45

There is another, also in C major, but in notes of half the value, with the heading 'La gaîté'. The theme in its final form has extraordinary beauty and subtlety; it is introduced by two bars which go through the most obvious modulation, from E♭ major to A♭ major through a dominant seventh, in an un-forgettable way, with a rhythmic ambiguity that gives a strange sense of mystery to the entry of the theme; this is in-tensified by the very Beethoven-like way in which the bass moves to the note of the tonic later than would be expected. The harmonic scheme of the theme is almost as simple as that of the Andante from Op 18, No 5 and has none of the un-expectedness of the Allegretto theme of the Finale of Op 74. It is in two strains of eight bars in which the melodic interest is shared between the first violin and the cello. The first modu-lates to the dominant, and the second consists of a phrase of four bars which is repeated. Finally there is a codetta of two bars in which the harmony is slightly more chromatic. The flowing 12/8 time inevitably suggests the 'Benedictus' of the Mass in D major and there is something of the same almost unearthly serenity. It continues throughout the first variation, which keeps closely to the outline of the theme, with greater rhythmic variety, and harmonic and contrapuntal details of extraordinary beauty; in some ways it is reminiscent of the first variation of the Arietta of Op 111. One of the first musicians to appreciate these late quartets was Mendelssohn; in a letter he describes how, when in a state of acute irritation, he gradually calmed himself by repeatedly singing the sweeping cadential phrase with which the second strain of this variation ends.

The second variation, in common time, is a dialogue for the two violins, antiphonal rather than contrapuntal, against a simple harmonic background; in both strains the second half is more animated than the first and in the second strain the codetta appears at the end of both halves. The general mood

anticipates that of the Andante con moto of Op 130. The
change from this to the third variation is brought about by
an enharmonic modulation of daring simplicity; the bare
octaves and the rising third give a sense of awe and expecta-
tion that is strongly reminiscent of the introductory bar of the
Adagio of the Piano Sonata, Op 106. The third variation, in
E major, is a kind of simplification of the theme. Though there
is no thematic resemblance, it has a decided similarity to the
theme of the Finale of the Piano Sonata in E, Op 109, not only
in the serene tenderness of its general mood, but especially in
the very impressive C♮'s in the bass that occur in both strains.
The second half of each of these contains some of the most
ethereal music that Beethoven ever wrote:

Ex 46

The change back from E to A♭ is smoother but no less effective
than the modulation that introduced the third variation. It
also brings back the 12/8 time, and the fourth variation,
though it begins with a new melody, is on the whole nearer to
the theme than any of the others. There are some new and
telling harmonic changes, but after the fourth bar the outline
of the theme is practically unchanged and the background of
repeated chords sometimes decorated by trills, very simple in
itself, is curiously exciting after the stillness of the preceding
variation. The rest of the movement may be considered an
extended coda. First there is a deeply thoughtful passage,
derived from the first four notes of the theme and modulating

mysteriously through D♭ major and C♯ minor in a texture far
barer than anything else in the movement. This is followed by
a luxuriously ornate variation of a shortened version of the
theme, with flowing semiquavers similar to those in the Adagio
of the ninth symphony. During the last nine bars of the movement E major, the key of the third variation, appears for a
moment like a far distant view; the final cadence:

Ex 47

like that of the first movement, is very unceremonious but
totally convincing and leaves the same feeling of repose as the
rather similar end of the first movement of the Piano Sonata
in A major, Op 101.

The third movement, Scherzando vivace, is large in scale
and elaborate in detail, but simple in its general plan. The
persistent dotted-note rhythm of its main section recalls the
third movement of Op 95, but its drily humorous, conversational mood is much more akin to that of the second movement
of Op 59, No 1, though there is more counterpoint and less
lyrical relief. The all-important main theme is equally convincing when inverted melodically; in an early sketch the
dotted-note rhythm does not appear and it is oddly typical of
Beethoven that here, as in several other instances, a theme
should originally have been conceived without its most
striking and most obviously memorable feature. Though this
part of the movement is in terse binary form it has no contrasting second theme; the brief successions of three-bar

phrases that occur at the end of each half and the capricious Allegro passages in duple time in the second half are the only moments at which the dotted-note rhythm is not present. It continues quietly through the very attractive coda-like passage that leads from the end of the second half of the Scherzo to the Trio. This is in a far quicker tempo and its general plan is similar to that of the equivalent passage in the Piano Trio, Op 97. In both there is a vivid contrast between a mysteriously whispering theme in the minor and an aggressively hilarious theme in the major which appears three times, in different keys. But in the trio these appearances are preceded by long gradual *crescendi*, whereas in the quartet everything happens at a far more feverish pace. The key-scheme begins unconventionally with a modulation from E♭ minor to D♭ major; Beethoven had made a similar transition more gently in the third movement of Op 59, No 2 and on a much larger scale in the slow movement of the D major Piano Trio, Op 70, No 1 and in the Scherzo of the ninth symphony. At each of its reappearances the melody of the boisterous second theme covers an increasingly wide range; the last, in B♭ major, marks the climax of the Trio and is followed by a gradual *diminuendo*. This, again, recalls the equivalent passage in the Scherzo of the ninth symphony; in both movements, also after the *da capo*, Beethoven makes an elaborate feint at repeating the Trio and then brushes it aside abruptly after a few bars. The final notes of the Scherzo of Op 127 are reminiscent of the vivid imitation of a donkey's bray, 'hihiya', that occurs at the end of a comic part-song written by Beethoven many years previously for the corpulent violinist Schuppanzigh, whose quartet gave the work its first performance, but this may be only a coincidence. The movement as a whole is the only part of Op 127 that gives full expression to the abrupt and capricious side of Beethoven's latest style and it stands out with remarkable effect against the lyrical beauty of its neighbours.

The Finale has many subtle and unexpected features but in general it is far more easily approachable than the preceding movement. It has sometimes been described as Haydnesque, and this is appropriate to its good humour and also to the way in which a lilting and leisurely tune of the kind generally associated with rondos is here used as the main theme of a movement in fully developed sonata form. It is preceded by a striking introductory phrase in octaves which plays a less important part than might have been expected, though it makes one very effective reappearance. It is interesting to see how the tune, as originally sketched:

Ex 48

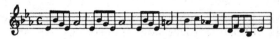

sat down in a curiously clumsy way in the fifth bar. A shorter but equally amiable tune follows, after which Beethoven, refusing to be hurried, returns to the main theme and uses its opening phrase as the basis of a beautifully coloured bridge passage. This leads to the second subject, which has a more decisive, march-like character; it culminates in a very strange phrase:

Ex 49

the startling harmony of which is modified in the recapitulation. Eventually the introductory phrase returns, but it leads, not to a return of the first theme, but to the development. In this, both main themes are used and towards the end there is a complete statement of the first subject, exquisitely scored, and of its sequel, in the subdominant. The recapitulation begins with an equally complete statement of both of these; this is characteristic of the leisurely atmosphere of the movement and contributes also to its curiously rondo-like impression. But its most striking feature is undoubtedly the long coda, which is one of Beethoven's strangest and most original. The modulation to the remote key of C major, brought about by raising the higher note of a trill, is magical; and the change of key brings with it a new and mysterious atmosphere, the main theme losing its comfortable lilt and turning into something much broader and more meditative. In the flowing triplets that surround it Beethoven luxuriates to an unusual degree in delicately sensuous colour, and after wandering through a typically Romantic succession of keys—C, A♭ and E—he returns very quietly and unobtrusively to E♭. The rest of the coda is devoted to the main theme in its new guise; it is presented against a variety of backgrounds, but always in close distance of the tonic and eventually the work ends with the greatest breadth and deliberation.

It is the combination of lyrical beauty with the harmonic and rhythmic subtlety of Beethoven's latest style that gives this quartet its peculiar individuality. It contains much, especially in the first and last movements, that makes a ready appeal even at a first hearing, and the meditations of the slow movement and the capricious high spirits of the Scherzo are more accessible to the listener than similar things in some of the later quartets. Its nearest equivalent among the last five piano sonatas is Op 110, but there the moods are more varied and possibly more direct in expression. But both works are among the most genial and approachable of Beethoven's third period, with only occasional glimpses of its more enigmatic and elusive features.

8

Op 132

THE difference of character between Op 127 and Op 132 is as marked as that between the first and second 'Rasumovsky' Quartets and it can be felt vividly in the slow introductions of their first movements. In the one the tonic is asserted boldly at the outset; in the other it is carefully avoided in a mysterious passage of eight bars. It was pointed out by Paul Bekker that the first four notes:

Ex 50

are related to the basic theme of the 'Grosse Fuge':

Ex 51

which was intended as the Finale of Op 130 and also, in a slightly different way, to the theme of the Fugue with which Op 131 opens:

Ex 52

On the strength of these facts he suggested that Beethoven had conceived the three works as a thematically connected triptych. In view of the fact that Beethoven was working at all three works at about the same time, the thematic resemblances are not surprising; some twenty years before he was haunted by a familiar and insistent rhythm which found its way into the fifth symphony, the 'Appassionata' Sonata and the fourth piano concerto. Then, where works of such different kinds were concerned, it can only have been a coincidence; in the case of the three quartets there is a possibility that the thematic connections might have been contrived deliberately, but it is far more likely that they came about subconsciously.

The Allegro of Op 132 breaks in abruptly on the introduction, which does not reappear in its original tempo. Its first four notes, however, in inversion, play a very important part as a counterpoint to the main theme:

Ex 53

and the combination of these two very dissimilar elements is one of the features that give the whole movement its strangely wayward character. They fit so easily that it is surprising to see from the sketch-books how long Beethoven took to find the ultimate form of the Allegro theme. The restless energy of the music recalls the Allegro con brio of Op 95, but here everything is laid out on a more spacious scale and the themes are for the most part developed at greater length. It is soon made clear that the second group is to be in the key of the submediant, as in Op 95, but Beethoven characteristically keeps the listener in suspense for some time before the arrival of its main theme. This is delayed, first by references to the first subject and then by an argumentative contrapuntal passage; at last it appears after an exciting *crescendo* and proves to be a charmingly lyrical tune of a rather Schumannesque kind. But, even in a movement of this size, Beethoven does not allow the lyrical mood to luxuriate, as a later composer would have done; it soon is made to give way to music of a more energetic character, though, again, there is a decided foretaste of Schumann in the cadence with which the exposition ends:

Ex 54

There are in Beethoven's works several first movements in which the traditional elements of sonata form are kept, but with unusual proportions. In that of the fifth symphony the coda is surprisingly long in view of the extreme terseness of the rest and this is still more pronounced in the first movements of the Piano Sonatas Op 81 and Op 101. In the A minor Quartet this process is carried a stage further. The exposition is not one of Beethoven's most extended, but it is long enough for the shortness of the development to come as a surprise. It begins with a reference to Ex 50, but is based for the most part on Ex 53. It moves quietly through G minor to C minor, but an emphatic cadence in that key is suddenly halted in mid-air by an enigmatic little phrase in C major which has no apparent connection with anything else in the movement and, for that reason, produces a strange feeling of remoteness. Soon Ex 53 returns and moves into E minor; again an emphatic cadence is interrupted, this time by a no less emphatic appearance of

Ex 50, which contrasts startlingly with its mysterious and sub-dued behaviour in the introduction and at the beginning of the development. But it soon subsides into its more normal rôle, that of the less obtrusive element in Ex 53. E minor is by now firmly established and it is in this key, the dominant, that Beethoven, most unusually, begins the recapitulation, the second group eventually appearing in C major. It follows the course of the exposition fairly closely, but there are some new features, such as the delicately decorative variations on the melody of Ex 53 and the subtly enriched scoring of the main theme of the second group. And finally, having ended the recapitulation in an extraneous key, Beethoven is faced with the problem of restoring the tonal balance by writing an extended coda.

Inevitably, this is throughout in the tonic, but it presents for the third time all the main features of the movement in such a way as to provide a fitting climax to it. A broad and thoughtful presentation of Ex 53 is followed by a new phrase:

Ex 55

which becomes increasingly prominent towards the end of the movement. The contrapuntal dialogue which led to the second group in both exposition and recapitulation appears again; the main melody of the second group itself is now in A major, with more changes in its scoring and deprived of its first three notes, giving it a curiously fleeting and dreamlike impression. No reference is made to the final stages of the group, but the all-important Ex 53 returns with new melodic variations against a restless background of semiquavers that almost certainly is derived from Ex 55; we are also reminded of the menacing double-dotted rhythm with which that phrase begins. The final appearance of Ex 53 seems to sum up in four bars the fiercer and gentler aspects of the movement:

Ex 56

It then gives place to the semiquavers of Ex 55 which, beginning quietly, soon surge up to a defiant and emphatic conclusion. The movement as a whole is exceptionally original; the problems resulting from its unusual proportions and tonal scheme are handled with marvellous imaginativeness and its tragic intensity is tempered by a streak of peculiarly appealing lyricism.

It appears from Beethoven's sketch-books that he had difficulty in deciding on the material for the second movement. Several ideas were jotted down and rejected; they include the tune afterwards used for the 'Danza alla tedesca' of Op 130 and another:

Ex 57

which reappeared in a startlingly different form in the slow movement of Op 135. Eventually he decided upon a pair of themes, one of which shares with Ex 50 the unusual feature of beginning on the leading note of the scale. They are treated with great persistence and frequently combined contrapuntally; Roger Fiske, writing in the Pelican *Chamber Music*, draws an interesting parallel between this movement and the Minuet from Mozart's Quartet in A major, K. 464, which has something of the same air of elegant, perhaps slightly aloof concentration. Some of Beethoven's contrapuntal clashes, e.g.:

Ex 58

recall the passage from Op 18, No 6, quoted as Ex 10; the casual way in which he modulates to and from C major, on the other hand, is essentially a characteristic of his latest manner. The central section is far more relaxed; in the charming passage over a drone bass with which it begins and ends, Beethoven is luxuriating in the delights of colour, much as Borodin did in the equivalent passage in the Scherzo of his Quartet in A major. The rest of this section is adapted from an Allemande in A major for piano which is thought to have been written about 1800. It is subtly and ingeniously done; the second strain of the Allemande, slightly altered, is introduced before the first:

Ex 59

which, when it eventually appears, is given a new character by
being shifted forward a beat. It is significant that, even at this
late stage in his career, Beethoven was able to use material
from a much earlier work without any feeling of incongruity. After an unexpectedly brusque phrase which contains a reference, probably unconscious, to the opening
fugal theme of Op 131, the musette-like passage returns;
finally there is a *da capo* of the main section of the movement.

The 'Heiliger Dankgesang' that follows is the strangest piece
of music that Beethoven ever wrote, and this strangeness is
emphasised by the fact that it comes between the quietly precise end of the previous movement and a prosaically vigorous
march. But its most notable features all have precedents in
earlier works. Its form, consisting of variations on two alternating themes, had been frequently used by Haydn and twice
before by Beethoven himself; first in the epigrammatic second
movement of the Trio in E♭ major, Op 70, No 2 and, on a far
larger scale, in the Adagio of the ninth symphony. Its composition was inspired by the recovery from an illness, but there
are suggestions of a similar programme in the Finale of the
Piano Sonata in A♭ major, Op 110, which was written after a
period, if not of physical illness, at least of profound emotional
stress resulting from the troubled relationship with his nephew.
Finally, its most unusual feature, the contrasting of a modal
with a classical tonality, had appeared in the 'Incarnatus' of
the Mass in D major, when, at the words 'Et homo factus est',
a mysterious Dorian D minor gives place to a warmer and
more human D major. Both here and in the third movement of
the A minor Quartet Beethoven uses a modal tonality not as
something to be incorporated into his ordinary musical
language, but to produce an atmosphere of mysterious and
other-worldly remoteness, which is to be contrasted with
something more normal. In the quartet the contrast is more

apparent, owing not only to the greater length of the movement but also to the alternating of the two elements that is demanded by its form.

As in the slow movement of the ninth symphony the two alternating themes are so spacious in themselves that there is room only for one variation of each, after which there is a long coda. The first is a simple chorale-like melody in five strains, each of which is played in simple block harmony, but is preceded by a smoothly polyphonic phrase. The Lydian tonality is far more uncompromisingly modal than anything in the sixteenth century, there being no hint of *musica ficta*; on the other hand the harmonies are more varied. The music has a strange, remote quality for which it would be hard to find any parallel, though there are passages in Sibelius's sixth and seventh symphonies that approach it. The opening of the slow movement of Bartók's third piano concerto is similarly planned, but there the atmosphere of the music is more romantic. For all its simplicity Beethoven's chorale melody is highly organised. The first strain, as so often in his tunes, moves only by step and lies within a narrow range. The second is larger in compass but contains no interval wider than a third. The next opens with a rising sixth, the widest leap, and ends on D, the highest note of the whole tune. The fourth has the largest compass, containing two descending fifths, and the last begins similarly but ends not on F, the final of the mode, but on E, preparing the way for the modulation to D major, the key of the second theme. The avoiding of a cadence at the end of the first theme is very characteristic of Beethoven's latest period, when he was increasingly anxious to obscure the familiar formal landmarks; he had done the same at the equivalent moment in the Adagio of the ninth symphony. The extraordinary continuity of the whole passage is further intensified by the polyphonic phrases; there are thematic relationships between the second, third and fourth and also between the first and fifth. The harmony is sufficiently plain for the dominant sevenths, when they appear, to have an effect of peculiar tenderness and for the inversions of the common chord to sound remarkably rich.

The transition from this to the second theme, which is headed 'Neue Kraft fühlend', is electrifying. For Beethoven the key of D major usually suggests a feeling of warmth and richness, especially when it appears in the course of a movement that is in another key; the slow movements of the Cello Sonata in D major, the ninth symphony and the 'Hammerklavier' Sonata all contain magnificent instances. Here the atmosphere is more robust, with exhilaratingly wide leaps in the melody and a brilliantly sonorous texture. Beneath much vivacious detail the section is clearly and broadly planned; there are two strains, each followed by a varied repeat, and then a codetta of great beauty, marked 'cantabile ed espressivo', which has a simpler melodic line than the rest and produces a wonderful sense of repose after the very exciting end of the second strain. After this a single chord of C major leads quietly and unceremoniously back to the Lydian tonality. On the face of things, neither theme seems particularly promising material for variations. The serene stillness of the first could easily be spoilt by clumsy elaboration and the second has in itself so much detail that any kind of variation seems hardly possible. Beethoven keeps the chorale melody of the first theme unaltered, but puts it an octave higher; a certain amount of gentle syncopation both in the contrapuntal phrases and under the chorale provides an increase of movement and some effective suspensions, but the atmosphere of Olympian contemplation remains undisturbed. The variation on the second theme is at first less ornate than the original but grows increasingly lively, the codetta losing some of its restful character; this emphasises all the more the extraordinary feeling of timelessness that permeates the last Lydian section.

It is built solely on two elements, the first strain of the chorale and a new, still more syncopated version of the first contrapuntal phrase (all three versions of it are shown in Ex 60):

Ex 60

The texture is very elaborate, both phrases being worked contrapuntally, either with themselves or with each other, and the part-writing is liable to produce surprising harmonic clashes. Even the strain of the chorale is represented at first only by its first five notes, though eventually the whole phrase is used. But it is the third version of Ex 60 that plays the most important part, floating mysteriously and elusively from one instrument to another; apart from a very brief modulation to D minor the Lydian tonality is maintained without any accidentals. The colouring is exquisitely graded; for the most part it is delicate and subdued, but towards the end there is a massive climax in which motion is reduced to a minimum and the atmosphere of rapt contemplation looks back to the Adagio of Op 59, No 2. The Lydian tonality is fascinatingly ambiguous, constantly veering towards C yet restrained by a quietly persistent pull towards F. In the last stages of the movement C almost prevails but at last it gives place to a chord of F major which, as in so many sixteenth-century works, sounds all the more inevitable for having been postponed for so long.

After the ethereal end of this movement a sudden jerk down to earth seemed to be the only possible continuation. A rather similar situation occurs in the Piano Sonata in A major, Op 101, where a particularly tender and intimate first movement is followed by a curiously angular and rather crabbed march. In the A minor Quartet the descent is from an even loftier height and the march to which it leads is simpler and more aggressively earthy. But it has unusual features, especially in the second half, in which the main theme reappears unexpectedly soon and then shows an odd tendency to hark back to the key of the dominant from which the music has only just returned. A few bars based upon the last three notes of the march lead to a sudden outburst of recitative played by the first violin against a background of tremolo. There are four works by Beethoven in which passages of this kind occur, the other three being the ninth symphony and the Piano Sonatas in D minor, Op 31, No 2 and A♭ major, Op 110. In all four the phrases are of a very similar kind, consisting largely of familiar clichés and, probably for that very reason, they evoke vividly the atmosphere of opera and produce the feeling of suspense resulting from the unexpected entry of a character from some other sphere. It is possible, as Dr Fiske has suggested in his *Musical Pilgrim* booklet on the posthumous quartets, that the recitative in Op 132 may have some connection with the fact that the theme of its Finale was originally intended for the ninth symphony. It ends with a familiar cadential formula, slightly modified so as to anticipate subtly the accompanying figure of the theme of the Finale.

This, like many of Beethoven's finest tunes, did not come into existence easily. Ex 61 shows an early version of it in

D minor, sketched at the time when it was intended for the
ninth symphony:

Ex 61

The very persistent rhythm looks back to the Finale of the
Piano Sonata in D minor. In the final version the greater
rhythmic flexibility gives the tune a far more sweeping and
compelling character and the repeated notes which bring Ex 61
to a rather pedestrian end are so much more effective when
transferred to the fourth and fifth bars. The second strain of
the tune in its final form is also an improvement on the early
sketch, which already contained a rising sequence, but was
much less urgent owing to its rhythmic similarity to the first
strain. With all its sombre and passionate character, the tune
in its eventual version is more suited to the intimate atmosphere
of a string quartet than to a work of the monumental nature
and dimensions of the ninth symphony. It is also particularly
suited to the spacious sonata-rondo form of the Finale of
Op 132. After a leisurely exposition of the main theme, in
which both strains are played twice, with slight modifications,
Beethoven moves quickly to the first episode, which is equally
impassioned but more short-winded and soon leads back to a
complete return of the theme, the last two bars of which form
the basis of the second episode. This is restless and agitated,
with frequent cross-rhythms of the kind that are so frequently
used by Brahms when writing in triple time; this movement
may well have influenced the Finale of his string quartet in the
same key. But the return of the main theme after the second
episode could hardly have been devised by anyone but Beet-

hoven in his latest style; for several bars it toys with the idea of returning in the key of D minor, the subdominant, and then at the very last moment decides after all to do it in A minor, with so casual an air that the listener is hardly aware, at the time, of what has happened. After a recapitulation in the tonic of the first episode the main theme makes its final appearance; this time it is prepared at considerable length and eventually returns in a quicker tempo. It does not quite complete its course, however, but goes unceremoniously into A major for a long coda. This contains occasional references to the theme but there is also a certain amount of new material; the general atmosphere is far more light-hearted, yet somehow it does not sound irrelevant. About halfway through it seems to be on the point of ending, but then to change its mind, with the result that all the earlier part of the coda is repeated with slight alterations of detail. The final bars are extended, an unexpected C♮ in the bass producing for a moment a strangely hollow effect just before the end.

This Finale provides a magnificent climax to one of the most intimate and withdrawn of Beethoven's works. Of all the posthumous quartets it is the slowest to reveal its secrets. The unusual proportions of the first movement and the almost hypnotically persistent treatment of the main theme of the second movement show Beethoven in a wayward mood in which he is less than ever inclined to come to meet his audience, and in the 'Heiliger Dankgesang' he soars still further away into his own imagination, exploring a strange and solemn region of his own discovering; coming after it the little march, for all its brisk and cheerful manner, sounds half ironical. But it is in the Finale, with its sweeping melody, that the music comes out finally into the open without in any way lowering the standard of inspiration. The key of A minor is not very common in Beethoven's music; perhaps the most familiar instances of it outside this quartet are the slow movements of the third 'Rasumovsky' Quartet and the seventh symphony, both of which express a kind of subdued and restrained melancholy, elegiac rather than passionate in character. But in the first and last movements of Op 132 the emotion is less restrained, though it does not suggest either the defiance and energy of C minor or the sombre brooding of D minor. And in the rest of the work there is a variety of mood and texture, not as extensive as in Op 130, but very remarkable—most note-worthy, perhaps, in the extraordinary contrasts between the alternating sections of the third movement, where the remotest contemplation and the most exuberant joy are put side by side with each other with a boldness hardly to be found elsewhere in Beethoven's music.

9

Op 130

IN its original form, ending with the 'Grosse Fuge', the Quartet in B♭ major, Op 130, held a position among the quartets similar to that of Op 106 among the piano sonatas, that of a towering colossus. No less remarkable than the size of the works as a whole was the disparity of size between the individual movements, ranging from the enormous proportions of the Finale to the extreme concision of the second and fifth movements. To those who believe firmly in the conscious thematic connection between Op 130, 131 and 132, the removal of the Fugue from Op 130 inevitably appears as a change for the worse, and coming after the Cavatina the opening theme of the second Finale has an almost disconcertingly flippant air, similar to that, in its context, of the Finale of the Piano Trio in B♭ major, Op 97. But there is another side to the picture. The Fugue, though no longer dismissed as an unintelligible freak, is a work of the utmost complexity, containing within itself all the contrasting elements that are characteristic of a full-length symphonic work in several movements; the very qualities that make it so impressive and satisfying as a separate work result also in its being, as the Finale of Op 130, disproportionately long and exhausting to the digestion of most listeners.

The first movement of the Quartet in B♭ major is at the same time very broad in its construction and very economical and closely wrought in the treatment of its themes. It has some

of the same feeling of intense concentration that Beethoven
had achieved, on a smaller scale and in a more tragic mood,
in the first movement of the Piano Sonata in C minor, Op 111.
The unusual plan of the exposition looks back to another,
much earlier piano sonata, Op 31, No 2 in D minor. In both
movements the slow opening bars recur, not only in the later
stages of the movement, but also during the course of the first
group and are included in the repeat of the first half. The
Adagio ma non troppo with which Op 130 begins is more
expansive and leisurely than the equivalent passages in Op 127
and Op 132 and the brief recurrence of the slow tempo after
only five bars of Allegro results inevitably in a spaciously
planned exposition. The main theme of the Allegro, like that
of the A minor Quartet, consists of the contrapuntal combination of two strongly contrasted elements:

Ex 62

The unexpected dynamic markings of this are very characteristic of Beethoven; equally so is his willingness, even at this
late stage in his life, to use as one of his main thematic ideas a
running figure that had already become a very familiar formula
and had played a prominent part in movements as dissimilar
as the Finale of Mozart's 'Jupiter' Symphony and the first
movement of his own Op 111. After a cadence in the tonic a
transitional passage based on a dactylic figure that had already
appeared in the introduction leads very gradually towards the
dominant and then moves very impressively into G flat for the
second group. As in Op 111, this opens with a short phrase of

great beauty which is only allowed to make a tantalisingly brief appearance. It is punctuated by the semiquaver figure from Ex 62, which becomes increasingly prominent towards the end of the exposition. A vigorous contrapuntal passage leads to a very broad and emphatic cadence; this is followed by a mysterious passage in octaves leading first to the repeat of the first half and then to the development section.

In view of the size of the whole movement this development is shorter than might be expected, but still more unusual is the fact that it contains the most relaxed music in the movement and has almost the air of being a kind of lyrical interlude. First there is a brief dialogue between the first two bars of the opening Adagio and Ex 62; then the last two notes of the former quietly detach themselves from the rest. Assisted by both elements of Ex 62 they form a background for a new theme:

Ex 63

which has no obvious connection with anything else in the movement, though attempts have been made to derive it from the opening of the second group. Starting in D major, the music wanders delightfully through various keys; after hesitating for a moment between C minor and C major it eventually chooses the latter, from which it returns abruptly to B♭ for the recapitulation. The opening Adagio plays no part in this; the semiquavers of Ex 62 are more exuberant than before and the tonality is more restless, leading through E♭ minor to

Db major. As in Op 111, the opening phrase of the second group is allowed to continue for slightly longer than in the exposition; it appears first in Db and then modulates to Bb with a wonderful lightening of colour. Equally beautiful are the harmonic differences between the Gb and Db versions of the phrase, both of which are quoted in Ex 64:

Ex 64

The rest of the recapitulation follows the exposition fairly closely. At the beginning of the coda the first four bars of the opening Adagio return, but, after a few bars of dialogue, reminiscent of the opening of the development, it gives way to Ex 62, which has the last word; the movement ends in a manner very characteristic of Beethoven, a hushed *pianissimo* being swept aside at the last moment by loud chords. It has not the passionate intensity of the first Allegro of the A minor Quartet nor the mellow lyrical grace of that of Op 127, and at first acquaintance it impresses more by individual moments than by its overall effect. Apart from Ex 64, the themes are woven with exceptional closeness into their context and the movement needs a patient approach for its full beauty and profundity to be appreciated.

By contrast the Presto that follows it makes so quick and ready an appeal that it may on first hearing seem slighter than it really is. Beethoven's immense capacity for building on a large scale has sometimes blinded his admirers to his equally great gift for saying much in a small space. In this movement, engagingly clear and simple in its themes, he has produced a fascinating miniature, with curious undercurrents of mystery and boisterousness. It is in a very clear-cut ternary form, the central section being rather unexpectedly long. The lively main theme is at first stated in a whisper; in its second half there is an unconscious recollection of one of the tunes of the Finale of the G major Piano Concerto. In the central section a one-bar figure is repeated with a persistence worthy of a Bach prelude; the suppressed energy of the main section here becomes more overt. It is followed by a very odd passage in which descending and mostly chromatic scale passages alternate with gruff anticipations of the return of the first section; this is restated in full with written out and delightfully varied repeats. The coda casts a final glance back to the main theme, recalled very quietly by the viola, and it then ends with a characteristically abrupt *forte*. Apart from the more robust central section the texture is particularly delicate and subtle. The whole movement is a masterpiece of imaginative understatement; its liveliness and rhythmic energy make a quick and ready appeal, but behind these are half-shades that are all the more impressive for being no more. The second movement of the Piano Sonata in A♭ major, Op 110, and the Bagatelle in B minor from Op 126 both foreshadow its mood to some extent, but there the energy is more aggressive and here it is more veiled and mysterious. Apart from its intrinsic qualities, this movement is particularly effective in its context, coming between one of the largest and most elaborate of Beethoven's first movements on one side and a delightfully leisurely and discursive slow movement on the other.

Among Beethoven's late works there are several instances of a slow movement opening with a few introductory bars leading from the key of the preceding movement. The most remarkable is in the Piano Sonata in B♭ major, Op 106, where the first two notes of the Adagio, added after the rest, serve the double purpose of bridging the very wide gulf between B♭ major and F♯ minor and also of establishing a thematic connection with the two preceding movements. In the ninth symphony and the Quartet, Op 127, the distance between the two keys is in both cases much shorter, but the journey is taken with so much breadth and deliberation as to give the feeling that something of the greatest significance has been accomplished. The third movement of Op 130 also has two introductory bars, but here there is no hint of solemnity. They are marked 'poco scherzoso' and the playfulness takes the form of keeping the hearer in doubt, until the last half-beat of the second bar, whether the music is in B♭ minor, the key of the preceding movement, or D♭ major; they also anticipate the main theme. The dark, rich colouring often associated by Beethoven with the key of D♭ has no place in this movement; the texture is delicate and the general atmosphere one of pleasant busyness, with frequent touches of the fantastic and unexpected. The main theme was originally sketched in notes of double the length, which suggests that the pace should be very moderate; at the same time the fact that two bars of the sketch become one in the eventual version is a reminder that the phrasing should be broad and the pace not so slow as to blur the general outlines of the music.

In his later works Beethoven did not often use sonata form for slow movements; the only instance in the last five piano sonatas is the great Adagio of Op 106, where it appears at its most spacious, with a development section that, though short in comparison with the other parts of the movement, is of great significance. After Op 59, Nos 1 and 2 there is no slow movement in full sonata form among the Quartets, but the Andante of Op 130 uses it without a development and with unusual proportions. The first theme occupies only seven bars, ending with a very precise cadence. A single bar leads from this to the second group, which is far longer and rambles happily in an almost Schubertian manner. Beginning in A♭ major, the dominant, with a simple and clear-cut tune, it soon wanders off into remote keys and at one point the first theme reappears for a moment and is treated canonically. Eventually the music returns to A♭, leading to one of the most haunting phrases that Beethoven ever wrote:

Ex 65

This is treated at some length, but just as it seems to be on the point of a decisive cadence a subtle reminiscence of the introductory bars quietly leads the music back to D♭ for the recapitulation. Apart from a slightly more energetic accompaniment figure for the main theme, this is fairly regular, the second group reappearing in the tonic. But Ex 65 soon wanders into a long and very imaginative coda. Phrases from the main theme lead to a mysterious chromatic passage almost Wagnerian in its flavour; then a reminiscence of the introductory bars is followed by a singularly beautiful canonic sequence built on the first phrase of the main theme. Features of the second group are also recalled and after an odd moment of suspense Ex 65 makes a final appearance. The movement ends with two highly exhilarating bars which have something of the exuberance of the Andante sections of the third movement of Op 132, but in a more playful and light-hearted mood. The

E

gaiety of this music, though capricious at times, has none of the brusqueness that often characterises Beethoven's more hilarious moments. It is a wholly delightful movement and behind its charm there is a warm tenderness that becomes more apparent the better it is known.

The general scheme of this enormous quartet is carefully balanced, the first movement being followed by the shorter and tenser of the two scherzos and then the longer and more relaxed of the two slow movements. In Beethoven's day the gulf between serious and popular music was far smaller than it is now, and even in as late a work as Op 130 it was possible for him to introduce a movement described as 'alla danza tedesca' without the element of irony that characterises similar passages in the music of Bartók. The theme of this movement was originally sketched in A major for the Quartet in A minor and, as Tovey pointed out, its first two bars are, by an odd coincidence, an inversion of the opening of the first movement of the Piano Sonata, Op 79, which is headed 'Presto alla tedesca'. The rhythm of the dance is here conveyed without the aid of the conventional waltz accompaniment and one of the charms of the movement is the contrast between the simplicity of the tunes and the unobtrusive subtlety with which they are presented. The harmonic background of the main theme is of the plainest, but the persistent quaver movement of the bass part is liable to lead to an unexpected inversion. In the central section a very simple tune is repeated several times, first in G major and then in C major, against an increasingly rich contrapuntal background; then two phrases from the tune detach themselves from the rest and are heard alternately, with an almost hypnotic persistence. When, after this, the main theme makes a very casual and completely unprepared return, the effect is almost that of a shock. The rest of the movement is devoted mainly to an elaborate repetition of the first section, with variations, sometimes of

the tune and sometimes of the inner parts. There is a coda,
during the course of which fragments of the tune, unhar-
monised, are tossed inconsequently from one instrument to
another; in the closing bars the final tonic chord is postponed
to the last possible moment in a manner very characteristic of
Beethoven's latest style:

Ex 66

And the fact that the thematic material of this movement
could easily have been composed during the eighteenth century does not mean that the movement as a whole has an
archaic effect; at no time in his life was Beethoven too self-
conscious to use the melodic idiom that he had heard in his
youth.

The longer and more relaxed of the two scherzos is followed
by the movement, the composition of which, according to
Beethoven himself, moved him more deeply than that of any
other of his works. But it can be seen from the sketches that
the tune did not come to him easily. Ex 67 shows that the
beautifully overlapping phrases which in the final version are
divided between the two violin parts were originally conceived
as a continuous melodic line:

Ex 67

In Ex 68 the melody is much nearer to its eventual form, but with a more obvious and less telling climax:

Ex 68

The rising phrase—Bb, D, Eb, F—at the equivalent moment in the final version recalls the slow movements of the Piano Sonatas, Op 106 and 109; it was noted as a characteristically aspiring 'Beethoven fingerprint' by Ernest Newman in his book, *The Unconscious Beethoven*, but its significance had been observed some years earlier in J. M. D. Rorke's *A Musical Pilgrim's Progress*. The total impression of the Cavatina, like that of the first movement of Op 101, is of such unbroken continuity that when hearing it one is hardly conscious of any formal landmarks, but its design has several unusual features. When the main theme has run its course, the opening bars return and lead to a dialogue built on the first bar of Ex 67, which appears to be moving to another key but instead leads to the last thing that would be expected at this stage, a new theme in the tonic. This is a passage of extraordinary directness and simplicity; it is firmly rooted in its key and contains a considerable amount of quasi-repetition, but always with subtle variations of melody or harmony. It is in this part of the movement, in particular, that one is most conscious of its affinity, rightly pointed out by d'Indy, with the Adagio of the ninth symphony. Not only is there the same feeling of what might be called serene intensity, but also a similarity in the cadences and in the way in which they are echoed. After the deeply restful end of this section the change to Cb major, the first real modulation in the movement, gives exactly the sense of oppression suggested by the direction 'beklemmt'. Perhaps the most extraordinary thing about the episode that follows is the fact that, for all its atmosphere of foreboding, it lasts for only seven bars. It is not so much the melody or the harmony that gives it its unique character, but the strange rhythmic contrast between the broken phrases played by the first violin and the pulsating triplets beneath them. The tension soon seems to collapse in exhaustion, after which the return to the main theme is marvellously contrived. In the first bar of Ex 69 the chord of E♭ is felt as the dominant of A♭ minor, but the harmony of the next bar, especially the rising bass on the second beat, makes it quite clear that the music has now returned to the home-key and it also dispels beautifully the dark and sultry atmosphere of the preceding passage:

Ex 69

After the first theme has returned with slightly modified harmony there is a coda in which the first bar of Ex 67 is again treated imitatively, though it is never, at any stage in the movement, given to the first violin. The final cadence looks back to the passage that precedes the modulation to C♭ major; in the last two bars the entry of the first violin has an effect of indescribable peacefulness. Of the overwhelming depth of the Cavatina there have never been two opinions, but, like the Adagio of Op 74, writers have reacted to it in different ways;

some have felt it to be a profoundly tragic piece of music, while others have stressed its serenity, or its religious fervour. Perhaps, in the long run, the most satisfying description can be found in the simple words of d'Indy: 'A masterpiece of melody.'

Of the first five movements of this work the Cavatina undoubtedly provides the culminating point, and even for a Beethoven the task of finding a suitable successor to it cannot have been easy. After the first performance of the work the enormous fugue with which it originally ended was generally thought to be too long and Beethoven allowed himself to be persuaded to publish it separately; the second Finale, written some months later, was his last composition, but, in defiance of chronology, it will be examined here before its much larger predecessor. Its first sketch:

Ex 70

has no resemblance whatever to the eventual theme and it is impossible to predict how it would have developed. It is interesting that Beethoven eventually opened this Finale on the same note, G, with which the 'Grosse Fuge' had begun. The atmosphere, however, is totally different and is equally far removed from the monumentality of the Fugue and from the romantic conception of a swan-song. The main theme is a cheerfully matter-of-fact tune, accompanied by a lively hopping figure; it pretends in its first four bars to be in C minor, anticipating a similar device in the Finale of Schubert's last piano sonata in the same key. The general character of this opening leads one to expect a rondo, but, as often in Haydn's music, the movement proves to be an elaborate structure, approximating to sonata form, but with very unusual features. Its exposition ends in F major, with a second group that is full of ideas, though with no very outstanding theme. But early in the development there is, most unexpectedly, a lyrical episode in A♭ major, with a melody of great distinction:

Ex 71

This is recalled, though not quoted note for note, by Borodin in the first movement of his Quartet in A major. The texture here is at the same time simple and very sonorous, the melody being for the most part doubled in octaves.

After this very delightful interlude the development proceeds with a long and elaborate fugal passage in which a fragment of the main theme is worked against an indefatigable counterpoint in semiquavers. Eventually this leads to a powerful passage in octaves, after which the first theme returns cautiously, at first in the wrong key and going through G minor and E♭ major. Finally it settles in B♭ major and the recapitulation goes its way with the second group returning in the tonic. This is followed by an extremely long and eventful coda. The lyrical episode returns, at first in E♭ major but soon moving to B♭; the rest of the movement is devoted to the first theme, which undergoes an infinite variety of treatment, many of its individual features being developed independently of others; the hopping accompaniment figure also plays an important part. There is an exciting *crescendo* at the end of which the tune appears in a high register, beginning, as on two previous occasions, in E♭ major instead of C minor and the rhythmic energy of the last page is remarkable.

The long and elaborate peroration is of a kind more characteristic of Beethoven's middle period than of his last works, but it is magnificently organised, both in the use it makes of the various melodic features of the main theme and in its skilful grading of tension and dynamics. To the movement as a whole it gives an immense spaciousness and so far as dimensions are concerned there can be no suggestion of its being inadequate as a Finale to Op 130. But the ultimate choice between this movement and the 'Grosse Fuge' is bound to depend not only on the intrinsic merits of the two compositions, but on the more elusive question: is the sublime Cavatina best followed by the high spirits of the one or the extreme complexity of the other? A contrast of some kind is obviously called for and the answer to the question is bound to depend to some extent on individual temperament. Even in the matter of sheer musical merit the comparison is extremely difficult, as the two pieces of music are so widely dissimilar in their personalities. The second Finale has not the lyrical grace of the last movement of Op 127 nor the passionate sweep of that of Op 132, and on first acquaintance at least it may leave a rather impersonal impression. But, as in the decidedly similar Finale of the 'Archduke' Trio, a superficially flippant exterior conceals much that is highly characteristic and imaginative and with all its sonority it is superbly written for its medium. Beside the Olympian striving and monumental structure of the 'Grosse Fuge' it may seem insignificant, but it has already been suggested that the immensely varied moods expressed in the different sections of the Fugue are best appreciated if it is regarded, not as the Finale of an already very extended work, but as a separate composition of symphonic dimensions containing within itself the contrasts usually associated with the familiar three- or four-movement scheme.

10

Op 133

BEETHOVEN himself described his 'Grosse Fuge' as 'tantôt libre, tantôt recherché', and on the whole the first of these adjectives is the more significant. It would be impossible to expect a work of this size to maintain a strictly fugal texture throughout and the work is best understood if regarded, not as a highly eccentric fugue, but as a kind of symphonic poem consisting of several contrasted but thematically related sections and containing a certain amount of fugal writing. A few years before, Schubert, in his 'Wanderer' Fantasia, had devised a similar scheme, though there is no fugal writing until the final section, and there are a considerable number of instances of it in the works of later composers, including several of Liszt's symphonic poems; one of the most impressive twentieth-century specimens is Medtner's splendid and unduly neglected Sonata in E minor, Op 25, No 2.

The basic theme of the 'Grosse Fuge' has already been quoted as Ex 51; it was first sketched alongside the very similar opening phrase of the A minor Quartet. Later sketches show Beethoven trying out various counter-subjects for it. Some of these were discarded, but one of them was eventually used for the slow lyrical section in Gb major and two others:

Ex 72

Ex 73

show the gradual stages by which Beethoven eventually found
what he wanted:

Ex 74

They also illustrate a point already mentioned; the way in
which the most obviously striking features of a Beethoven
theme may be the last to arrive. Ex 72 has the general melodic
outline of Ex 74, but has neither the very wide leaps nor the
very distinctive rhythm; Ex 73 has the leaps but not the
rhythm.

The work opens with a short introduction beginning with
a powerful announcement of Ex 51 in the key of G major,
which was obviously intended to come immediately after the
end of the Cavatina; even those who feel that this work would
not have made an ideal finale to Op 130 may at the same time
admit that the opening slightly loses point when it is not
preceded by the E♭ major chord with which the Cavatina ends.

But, in any case, it at once creates a vivid atmosphere of suspense, presenting a kind of preview of the various shapes in which the main theme will appear, first bold and aggressive, as in Ex 51, then in a jaunty 6/8 rhythm that is used later in the Scherzo section.

Finally it is played by the first violin as it appears as theme A in Ex 74, but in a whisper. Then, after a pause, the first section of the Fugue begins with the very striking combination of themes shown in Ex 74. The way in which theme A goes to the note of the tonic at the last possible moment gives an odd harmonic twist very characteristic of Beethoven's latest manner. But all through this section, although theme A plays an important part, it is the wide leaps and insistent rhythm of theme B that dominate the music; for several pages on end the players are instructed to play *fortissimo* and the melodic lines are angular in the extreme. But behind the elaborate detail and uncompromising manner a firmly planned scheme can be traced. The exposition proceeds on normal lines; it is followed by a short episode, after which the two themes return with a new counterpoint in triplets. The intervals in theme B become more and more varied and with the increasing restlessness of the music the texture becomes less orthodox. At one point theme B is played by the viola and cello in tenths; theme A disappears from the scene and there is a furious passage built entirely upon various features of theme B.

After this tremendous outburst, however, its aggressive rhythm begins to lose its momentum. The next stage is marked by the return of theme A and by the appearance of a new counterpoint in dactylic rhythm; theme A appears in a different rhythmic position and theme B is never given in its entirety to any one part, but is divided between two instruments.

Soon both themes appear in diminution:

Ex 75

with theme B in a triplet rhythm that gives it a slightly less
aggressive character. Soon, however, it makes a final attempt
to assert itself in its original rhythm, in a very high register
and with enormously wide leaps. After two bars, however, this
is deflected by a sequential passage which modulates very
deliberately to G♭ major. At this point it is interesting to look
back and to discover that, with all its restlessness, the work
has so far moved within a very narrow range of keys. The
whole of this first section has a strange hectic quality which is
made all the more extraordinary by the fact that, when reduced
to its barest harmonic essentials, it is comparatively simple.
Beethoven seems to be struggling to some extent with the
limitations of the idiom of his day and, still more, with those
imposed by the medium of the string quartet. There is also a
sense of a struggle between the two themes; the broad and
deliberate outline of A and the energy and feverish leaps of B.

So far the more prominent part has been played by B, but
A has never been absent from the scene for long. It is significant, however, that its most aggressive feature, the trill on its
final note (see Ex 51), has not appeared since the opening bars
of the introduction. So far its personality seems to be that of
a foil to its far more self-assertive rival. The extreme technical
difficulty of the first section of the 'Grosse Fuge' undoubtedly
imposes a strain on both performers and listeners; this is much
less felt when it is played on a string orchestra, though some take
the view that, like Mussorgsky's 'Tableaux d'une Exposition',

the music loses some of its essential character when transferred to a smoother medium. But it is, for the most part, on the strength of its first ten pages that the words 'uncouth', 'rugged' or 'outlandish' have been applied to the work as a whole. When a difficult work is imperfectly known, its more uncompromising features often make at first a disproportionately deep impression and for many years the rough-edged quality of the first section of the 'Grosse Fuge' blinded many musicians to the wonderful beauty and serenity of the music that follows it.

The section in G♭ major, marked 'Meno mosso e moderato', brings with it a sense of blissful relaxation similar to that produced by the equally beautiful D major episode in the Finale of Op 106. Two introductory bars, based on a skilfully disguised version of the first four notes of theme A, lead to a quietly flowing melody:

Ex 76

which had made a very tentative appearance, as a countersubject to theme A, in the introduction; here, however, it enters in its own right, against a very simple harmonic background. Before long theme A enters and, combined with Ex 76, weaves a texture of the most ethereal kind, far removed from the tumult of the first section. It now seems an entirely changed personality; in the first section it was the staider and less aggressive of the two contrasted elements, but here, when combined with the suave diatonic phrases of Ex 76, its chromatic contours give a gentle edge to the music. At one point it is played in canon by the cello and the first violin, accompanied by fragments of Ex 76, but the serenest moment of all is when it is sung by the first violin in a very high register over a pedal note held by the viola, with the cello playing Ex 76.

Throughout this section the music never strays far from the tonic and for most of the time the *pianissimo* is as sustained as was the *fortissimo* of the first section. For a moment the calm is disturbed by a short *crescendo*; this does not last, but after a final appearance of Ex 76 in octaves, the ethereal atmosphere is destroyed, and a mysterious shimmering passage, prophetic of the trills that play so important a part at a later stage, leads to an abrupt modulation from G♭ major to B♭ major and from the sublime to the matter-of-fact. The G♭ section, though not particularly long on paper, gives a feeling of remarkable spaciousness, which makes the change of atmosphere particularly startling, and for that reason particularly characteristic of Beethoven in his more wayward moods.

The next section, marked 'Allegro molto e con brio', is a scherzo in all but name; it opens with theme A in a lively dance rhythm that was foreshadowed in the introduction, but at first there is no pretence of fugal writing. Before long, though, complications arise and theme A is soon heard in its original shape (Ex 51), combined with two counter-subjects that are both ingeniously derived from its first three notes:

Ex 77

Allegro molto e con brio

The most significant feature of this passage is the increasing prominence of the trill on the last note of the theme, which hitherto has not been heard since its appearance in the introduction. Then it lasted for only a crotchet's length; now it is increased to a dotted minim and becomes more and more aggressive. Soon the last three notes of A, with the trill, are detached from the rest and worked independently, the two counter-subjects continuing. Then there is a new counter-subject in quavers, also derived from the first three notes of A. By this time the music has become very restless, with remote and rapid modulations. The trills become longer and more menacing, often lasting for several bars and recalling certain passages in the Finale of the Piano Sonata, Op 106. The climax of this section comes with a high and very emphatic entry of theme A, played by the first violin and followed by a frenzied succession of trills, under which the cello and viola treat the first three notes of A in canon. The combination of these two strongly contrasted elements is extraordinarily impressive; eventually the trills are left for a few moments in sole possession, echoing each other and producing an atmosphere of sullen suspense, which is, however, broken by an unexpected modulation bringing a complete change of atmosphere.

This passage is not only of immense power in itself, but it also marks an important stage in the general design of the work; from this point onwards themes from the earlier sections begin to return. The first to reappear is theme B, which has not been heard since the end of the long first section. It is now in 6/8 time and accompanied by an extraordinary and hardly recognisable transformation of A:

Ex 78

Considering its vast dimensions the range of keys covered by the 'Grosse Fuge' is surprisingly small; much smaller than that of the Finale of Op 106. The remotest is G♭ major, the key of the second section; the Scherzo begins in B♭ major, but in its later stages gravitates round A♭ major or F minor, with a certain amount of digression. The combination of theme B and Ex 78, beginning in E♭ major, moves towards A♭ major. The first three notes of theme A appear in their original form and then, inverted, over a pedal-point, in a very impressive descending sequence. The key of A♭ major is now firmly established and the tempo slackens to Meno mosso e moderato. The material of the G♭ section returns not in its original ethereal texture, but in richly glowing colours; this is perhaps the warmest and most quickly appealing part of the whole work. Characteristically, however, Beethoven does not allow it to continue for long; a brief climax is halted in mid-air and subdued and mysterious references to the trills lead to a return of the playful opening of the Scherzo, in B♭ major.

The rest of the work consists of a coda of great spaciousness, in which the conflicts in some of the earlier sections seem to have been resolved into music of the utmost suavity and charm. After the jaunty tune of the Scherzo has run its course, the 6/8 rhythm continues, but far more smoothly and with a broader harmonic outline. Theme A appears in various shapes, sometimes divided between two parts; after a moment of great solemnity, in which it is played in high register over sustained harmonies, Beethoven seems for a few bars to be rousing himself for a big climax, but then to change his mind. Theme B and Ex 76 are recalled for a moment but are swept aside by theme A, in its original form, played majestically in octaves. But again it does not rise to the expected climax and is soon heard, once more, over solemn and sustained harmonies, this time with a long trill in the bass. This for a moment recalls the stormier moods of the Scherzo and is followed by other short

trills. At this stage of the work, however, the general atmosphere of the music is too serene for a recollection of this kind
to be more than a passing shadow. It soon gives place to a
passage of great clarity and simplicity, built on the two themes
A and B in their original combination, against a background
of repeated chords. The atmosphere is totally different from
that of Ex 74. There we are immediately aware of a sense of
conflict between two exceedingly different personalities; here
everything is lyrical and harmonious and its effect, coming at
the last stages of a highly eventful and dramatic work, is
curiously moving. Finally, having so perfectly rounded off his
enormous design, Beethoven ends unceremoniously, with a
few bars of matter-of-fact tonic and dominant.

In no other work did he assemble in a single continuous
movement such a variety of incident or show so much resource
in developing his material. The transformations of theme A
foreshadow the methods of Wagner, Liszt and many other
composers; on the other hand, the way in which fragments of
it are sometimes detached from and developed independently
of the rest looks back to Bach and further still to the treatment
of plainsong themes by composers of Masses in the fifteenth
and sixteenth centuries. The melodic resemblance between
theme A and the opening bars of Op 132 has been much
stressed by commentators; less obvious but perhaps more
significant is the similarity of harmonic outline between the
combination of themes A and B and the similarly contrasted
pair of themes with which the Fugue of the Diabelli Variations
opens. In both movements the chromatic outline of the lower
theme produces a restless intensity that is far removed from
sentimentality; in the various versions of theme A of the
'Grosse Fuge', with the exception of Ex 78, the harmonic
implications of the theme are kept unaltered, which makes all
the more remarkable the variety of the counter-subjects that
accompany it. It has often been pointed out, with some justice,

that for Beethoven counterpoint was not the instinctive medium for musical expression that it had been for Bach. But it should be borne in mind that in Beethoven's time any fugal writing could degenerate only too easily into a fluent but dull imitation of an earlier idiom, and that he himself refused to regard the writing of conventional, routine fugues as a vital form of composition. It has been suggested earlier in this book that his counterpoint was extraordinarily varied in character and sometimes, as in the second movement of the Quartet in C minor, was presented in the most graceful and light-hearted manner. In his late works it could be uncompromisingly rough and angular but also, as in the Finale of the Piano Sonata in A♭ major, Op 110, smooth and thoughtful. And in his largest works he sometimes seems to be making a deliberate contrast between the two types. In the Diabelli Variations there is the contrast between the suave and gentle Fughetta and the more aggressive Fugue; in the Finale of Op 106 the quiet episode in D major stands out in wonderful relief against its strenuous surroundings; and finally we can find the same contrast expressed with immense power and on the largest scale in the 'Grosse Fuge'. And as a further indication of the range of Beethoven's methods, even in a work of this kind, written at this period, there are several passages in which the ideas are played against a background of simple repeated chords.

11

Op 131

BEETHOVEN wrote only two works in C♯ minor, and it is curious that both the piano sonata, Op 27, No 2 and the quartet, Op 131, begin unconventionally with a slow movement, reserving a full sonata form for the Finale. It is also highly characteristic of Beethoven to write within a short time two fugues so astonishingly dissimilar as the 'Grosse Fuge' and the first movement of Op 131. In the former he extended the form to enormous dimensions, so as to include a bewildering variety of mood and incident; in the latter he achieved a different kind of spaciousness by maintaining on a very broad scale a mood of deep and unbroken thoughtfulness. Since the death of Bach and Handel fugues had usually been brisk and animated; sometimes full of suppressed excitement, as in the remarkable *sotto voce* fugal finales of some of Haydn's Op 20 quartets, and sometimes fierce and aggressive, as in Mozart's Fugue in C minor for two pianos. But it was left for Beethoven, in his Quartet in C♯ minor, to recapture the brooding and meditative atmosphere of Bach's fugue in the same key, from the first book of the 'Forty-eight'.

The subject (Ex 52), for all its simplicity, contains two separable elements, A and B, and there is hardly a single bar in the whole Fugue that does not contain one of these. After the exposition there is a dialogue based on A; then four notes from B take charge. After the very bare texture of the preceding dialogue, the music here sounds richer and in spite of a solitary entry of the subject less essentially fugal. Another dialogue-like passage built on A brings back for a moment the sparer texture, but an entry of the subject in diminution leads to a very rich ascending sequence based on a fragment of B. Hitherto, with the exception of the unusual answer to the subject in the exposition, the music has gravitated towards dominant rather than subdominant regions, but now it moves into A major. This is a moment of the most ethereal beauty, in which the subject, thanks to a simple rhythmic shift, seems to become a new character:

Ex 79

The last two bars then detach themselves from the rest and form the basis of a passage of delicate but subtly shifting colour that leads back very gradually to the final section. This begins with developments of the third bar of the subject in its original form; soon it goes into diminution and provides a background to a series of entries of the complete subject. The last of these, in the bass, is in augmentation, and produces an effect of the utmost spaciousness. The end of the Fugue is mysteriously inconclusive, the frequent D♮'s modifying the effect of the C♯ major harmony and preparing the way for the very unusual key of the next movement.

A bare description of its formal outline can give but little idea of the extraordinary profundity of this Fugue. The features and incidents that have just been enumerated merge into each other so gradually that it is not easy, except after many hearings, to realise what has happened. Its atmosphere is totally unlike that of any other of Beethoven's fugues. Perhaps the nearest approach to it can be found, on a much smaller scale, in the thirtieth of the Diabelli Variations, which has something of the same deeply brooding quality, expressed in a musical texture which is not strictly fugal, but contains a certain amount of counterpoint. In both, the emotion is less poignant than the more human melancholy of the slow movements of the 'Hammerklavier' Sonata and the Cello Sonata in D major, Op 102, No 2, and the subtly shifting tonality and the very sensitive chromaticism give a feeling of mystical otherworldliness. In the C♯ minor Quartet this is made more impressive by the wonderful continuity of texture and spaciousness of design. When writing the slow movement of Op 132, Beethoven portrayed a vivid contrast between remote contemplation and human joy; in the first movement of Op 131 the contemplation is perhaps less Olympian, but it is maintained unbroken throughout the movement.

There can be little doubt that Beethoven, as his style matured, became increasingly conscious of the effect that the first chord or note of one movement would have after the end of what preceded it. But in Op 131, for the first time since the Piano Sonatas of Op 27, he made it clear that he wished all the movements to follow after each other without a break. After the sombre end of the opening Fugue, the change to D major for the next movement is magical in its effect. To follow the Fugue with a movement in fully developed sonata form might run the risk of excessive solidity; on the other hand, a sequel of too frivolous a character would have produced a jarring anticlimax. The Allegro molto vivace compromises most successfully; it is in a highly compressed sonata form with no development and an engagingly naïve main theme, which produces an odd and curiously touching contrast to what has gone before it. In the Fugue the dynamics never rise above *forte* and in the second movement, despite a brief climax shortly before the end, the gaiety is subdued, and the direction *poco rit* at the seventh bar of the theme gives a curiously hesitant feeling to the tune; Beethoven is not yet ready for the wild hilarity of the 'Presto' Scherzo.

The proportions of this movement, as so often in Beethoven's late works, are unexpected. The theme is followed by a bridge passage that moves in a very leisurely way towards A major but then seems to lose itself on the dominant of F♯ minor. Then, very quietly and unexpectedly, the main theme appears for a moment in E major, from which it is easy to move to A. The second group consists of short and vivacious phrases which keep up an unbroken crotchet-quaver rhythm; the music is for a time firmly rooted in A major, but just as it seems about to settle on a cadence it floats quietly back to the tonic for the recapitulation. In this the original bridge passage is omitted. Instead, there is a digression, built on part of the main theme, to G major and E minor, enabling the second group to return in the tonic; it is not, however, preceded this time by the unexpected reference to the main theme. To compensate for the absence of a development section, the coda is quite long; the first theme appears first in the subdominant and then in the tonic, but a far more important part is played by the transitional theme which was omitted in the recapitulation. It rises to a climax in the most brightly coloured passage that has yet occurred in the whole work. For a moment Beethoven, as so often, seems unable to make up his mind whether to end loudly or quietly; eventually he decides on the latter course, with two very informal, almost furtive cadences. Despite the liveliness of its principal theme, the general impression left by this movement is oddly elusive. Its persistent crotchet-quaver rhythm looks back to the remarkable Finale of the Piano Sonata in E♭ major, Op 31, No 3, in which ideas of an almost comic triviality are treated with remarkable power and imagination. But in the present movement everything is far more withdrawn; only in the coda does the music come out into the open for a moment before disappearing. The original

sketch of the main theme is less unlike the eventual version
than is often the case with Beethoven, but it does not contain
the frequent repetitions of phrase that give the tune, in its final
form, its curiously haunting, nursery-rhyme-like character.

The very short section that follows was labelled by Beethoven
himself as No 3, but it has the effect of an improvisatory interlude between two movements. Its opening bars could have
come from the development section of a movement in sonata
form, but they are soon held up by a rhapsodical passage for
the first violin. The atmosphere is not as operatic as in the
passages mentioned earlier in connection with the Finale of
Op 132, but the opening of the first violin's phrase recalls one
of the recitative-like passages in the first movement of the D
minor Piano Sonata, Op 31, No 2 and in its final bars:

Ex 80

a familiar operatic formula is beautifully translated into the
language of chamber music. The next movement is a set of
variations. Reference has already been made to the remarkably
different ways in which Beethoven approached this form. If
the great Adagio of Op 127 has something of the same continuity as the Arietta that ends the Piano Sonata, Op 111, the
Andante of Op 131 approximates more to the Finale of the
E major Piano Sonata, Op 109. The theme consists of two eight-
bar phrases, both of which are repeated with slight differences;
simple and almost childlike both melodically and harmonically,
it could quite conceivably have been written by an older
composer, but in that case it would probably have occurred in

an Allegretto finale rather than a slow movement. Coming here, as the centre-piece of one of Beethoven's greatest works, it should be played at a pace which precludes the slightest suspicion of jauntiness in the opening phrases and allows suitable breadth for the beautifully timed rising crotchets in the second half. This increasing rhythmic breadth in its second half is perhaps the most distinctive feature of the theme, and an unusual trait of the whole set is the way in which the variations are not only very different from each other, but seem, in several instances, to change their character as they proceed. For the listener who does not know the work well this may easily give the effect of a rather puzzling restlessness, and can suggest that the variations are a good deal freer than they really are. It also results in a variety of texture that can sound bewildering after the way in which the melody of the theme, sometimes divided between the two violins, is at first presented against the plainest and simplest harmonic background.

In Beethoven's later sets of variations the first tends to be comparatively simple, often in a peculiarly direct and appealing way; the slow movement of the Piano Trio, Op 97, and the finales of the Piano Sonatas, Op 109 and 111 all have singularly lovely instances. In the Andante of Op 131 the first variation is more complex and more restless; during the first eight bars it moves from a dark to an ethereal colouring. In the repeat this colouring is maintained, with the texture more broken up; during the second half and its repeat the rhythm becomes increasingly vivacious and the harmonic details increasingly plentiful, but without essentially altering the outline of the theme. The second variation goes at a quicker pace and is generally simpler and more direct in its appeal; it has a very nearly unbroken background of detached chords, the effect of which is almost startling after the elaborately woven texture of the preceding variation. They also cause a slight shift of harmonic emphasis in the first few bars and in the repeat, but on the whole the outline of the theme can easily be traced in this variation. The melodic phrases, short at first, gradually grow longer, the second half consisting largely of widely ranging arpeggios which culminate in an emphatic passage in octaves. The progress here from a hesitating to a far more confident mood is clearly portrayed, and there are none of the enigmatic features that are found in some of the other variations.

The next, headed 'Andante moderato e lusinghiero', is one of the strangest. Directions of this kind are commoner at this stage than in Beethoven's earlier work, though less so than in the music of later composers such as Weber or Tchaikovsky. Sometimes they occur in passages where the music in itself would not lead one to expect them; it is surprising, for instance, to find the words *dolce* and *espressivo* applied to the main theme of the Finale of the Piano Trio, Op 97. In this variation the word *lusinghiero* (coaxing) may be regarded as an indication that the music, despite its austerely contrapuntal texture, should be played lyrically, not drily. The first eight bars consist of a canonic dialogue, marked *dolce*, for the viola and cello; in the repeat this is transferred to the two violins, the lower instruments providing a very simple background, mainly of semibreves and minims. The F♯ played by the viola in the ninth bar is an unexpected touch very characteristic of Beethoven's latest style, with its frequent tendency to obliterate formal landmarks. For the second half the viola and cello resume their canonic dialogue, which is now built on from the cadential trill with which the first half ended. The atmosphere is far more argumentative than in the first part of the variation; this is intensified in the repeat, when the two parts, contrapuntally inverted, are played by the first violin and cello, the second violin and viola joining in the discussion by doubling the two parts, either in tenths or sixths. During this process the colouring gets gradually lighter and at length merges magically into the completely different texture of the next variation.

Throughout the first half and its repeat it is possible to trace the melody of the theme; in the second, it has practically disappeared and even the harmonic outline is almost obliterated by the persistent canonic imitation. The counterpoint here does not involve the striking clashes and suspensions that occur in the rather similar fifth variation in the Finale of the E major Piano Sonata, Op 109; it is at the same time smoother and in a curious way more elusive and enigmatic.

The fourth variation is headed 'Adagio', but it has not the solemnity that Beethoven usually associates with this direction. It is in a pleasantly relaxed mood, with a swaying, almost dancelike rhythm and a delicately luxuriant texture that contrasts perfectly with what came before it. The first half and its repeat keep fairly near to the harmonic outline of the theme; the second is freer and, in its first four bars, produces an effect of great pathos by moving into the supertonic minor instead of the expected subdominant. The last bar of the repeat recalls, very happily, the opening bar of the variation. The fifth returns to the reticent mood of the third, but is very different in character. There is no counterpoint and very little melody, the harmonic outline of the theme being presented in an enigmatic syncopated rhythm of the kind often used by Schumann. In the second half the rhythmic ambiguity is increased by the fact the first four bars are extended to five; there are, however, suggestions of the melody of the theme. The mysterious simplicity of this variation gives it a strangely individual character and its laconic understatement makes it a remarkably effective interlude between the grace of its predecessor and the extraordinary depth of what follows it.

This final variation, perhaps the most moving section of the whole work, is simple in texture and once the unusual 9/4 rhythm has been grasped, it makes a very direct appeal. In its opening bars the melody of the theme:

Ex 81

appears in a modified form in the bass:

Ex 82

The tempo is again Adagio and this time in the deeply thought-ful mood that this direction usually implies with Beethoven. But, like most of the variations in this set, it changes its character as it proceeds. The first half is in simple block harmony, the plainness of which is modified by the quiet and wholly unsentimental use of the diminished seventh. But in the repeat the serene, almost cloistered atmosphere is slightly disturbed in the first four bars by a rhythmic figure played by the cello and headed *non troppo marcato*. In the second half this is slightly more prominent and in the repeat of the second half it is so persistent that it is clearly impossible for the variation to return to its original calm; instead it leads into the long and eventful coda. This opens with a series of rhapsodical phrases for all four instruments, the harmonic outline of which is, however, very similar to that of the first half of the theme and could well be the opening of a new variation; instead, however, its progress is arrested by a series of trills and the music floats quietly and deliberately into C major and the melody of the first four bars of the theme is played *dolce*, but at a slightly quicker tempo. This soon gives way to a return to the original key and pace, and the first half of the theme is played with the melody unaltered, but doubled in octaves against a rich harmonic background with trills that do not sound menacing, as in the 'Grosse Fuge', but give a strange sense of vastness. Soon there is another digression, similar to the first, but going this time into F major and returning, almost imperceptibly, to the last four bars of the theme. Characteristically, the final cadence is postponed for as long as possible, and it can be seen from the sketch-books that the few bars that follow it caused Beethoven agonies of indecision. There are twelve versions sketched, some marked 'besser' or 'meilleur', but all fairly similar, with the same wistful glance towards the key of the subdominant minor. Some of the sketches are slightly simpler and others slightly more complicated than the final version, and it is interesting to see not only Beethoven's great sensitiveness to detail, but also the difficulty with which he made his final choice. Composition for him was certainly not the impulsive and spontaneous process that it was for Mozart and Schubert.

A glance at the movement as a whole shows at once not only the great beauty but also the structural importance of the coda.

During the variations the melodic outline of the theme can be felt only occasionally. But in the rhapsodical phrases with which the coda opens it is subtly but unmistakably implied; this gives added point to the more open references to it in the digression to C major, which, in their turn, prepare most effectively for the very full and richly coloured presentation of the first half of the theme that follows. After the digression to F major the design of the coda is beautifully rounded off by the very skilfully contrived return to the final bars of the theme, after which the ethereal and unceremonious conclusion brings a feeling of singular pathos.

Reference has been made in an earlier chapter to the enormous variety of mood in the C♯ minor Quartet; the words 'simple, straightforward, perfectly intelligible' applied to it by Bernard Shaw may not seem to fit the whole work, but they are certainly appropriate to the Presto in E major which follows the variations. Here the high spirits which had a curiously tentative air in the second movement find far fuller and more uninhibited expression. If Haydn had lived to hear it, he might have thought it puerile or vulgar, but it contains some of his spirit and, with all its wayward hilarity, it does nothing as strange as the odd harmonic digressions and feints that occur in the Finale of Haydn's Piano Sonata in C major, No 50. Its form is very simple; that of a Scherzo with a Trio that occurs twice and makes an unsuccessful attempt to do so a third time. The main section has a single theme, the first bar of which is comically anticipated by the cello and frequently detaches itself from the rest. The Trio contains a succession of tunes of which the first, more even than that of the second movement, has the repetitiveness of a nursery rhyme and remains contentedly in E major. The others, in the subdominant, are hardly less child-like but are allowed less leisure; the last of them moves back into E, and a grotesque passage built on an augmentation of the first bar leads to the return of the Scherzo. If the Trio is examined in detail it can be seen that, for all its air of naïveté, each of its tunes has some thematic link with its predecessor and the placid flow of simple melody contrasts admirably with the more fiery and explosive atmosphere of the Scherzo. After the repeat of the Trio, the passage leading to the return of the Scherzo is slightly altered and in the last appearance of the Scherzo itself there is at one point a very impressive reduction of dynamics reminiscent of similar passages in the 'Harp' Quartet and the seventh symphony. When this has run its course, three of the tunes from the Trio are recalled for a moment, after which the movement ends with a coda based on the theme of the Scherzo and containing a rapid and exciting *crescendo*. The effect of the whole movement, with its brilliance and high spirits, is electrifying in its deeply thoughtful surroundings and seems to laugh good-naturedly at those who regard the posthumous quartets as an unfathomable mystery.

The three loud G♯'s that follow suggest that the music is returning to C♯ minor. As a result of this the chord of G♯ minor with which the next movement begins has a peculiarly poignant effect. The key is very rare in Beethoven's works and this Adagio, quasi un poco Andante, like the short Adagio in the Piano Sonata, Op 101, says much in a very small space; it has something of the same quiet intensity as the Cavatina from Op 130, but is simpler in texture and more melancholy in mood. The melody of the first phrase:

Ex 83

Adagio quasi un poco Andante

is said by Fétis to have been taken from an old French folk-song; the chord of E major at the end of the second complete bar of the quotation is a beautifully placed piece of colour which is made still more beautiful when the tune is played an octave higher and the E in the bass is approached by a rising sixth. In the second strain the texture is barer, the melody being divided between the three upper strings, the cello moving on the last beat of the bar in a manner very typical of Beethoven's latest period. Although the modulation from G♯ minor to C♯ minor is carried out slowly and deliberately, after an interrupted cadence of great beauty, the opening bars of the Finale come as a sudden shock.

There are several sketches of these, including one in 6/8 time:

Ex 84

beginning in F♯ minor. At the end of the sketch appear the words *später nach Cis moll,* which suggest that at that particular stage Beethoven was planning to have a main theme that, like that of the Finale of Op 59, No 2, began in an extraneous key to which it would constantly attempt to return. This is interesting in view of the fact that the two movements have the same persistently galloping rhythm, though, as was pointed out in an earlier chapter, its effect is far more sombre in the C♯ minor Quartet. For the first time in the work Beethoven uses fully

developed sonata form. Of two contrasting elements of the
theme in its eventual form:

Ex 85

the figure marked A is an earlier version of the opening phrase
of Ex 84; the other is not found in the earliest sketches, but
first appears in Ex 84 in 6/8 time. These two strongly marked
ideas play the most important part in the movement, but there
are others of a gentler character. The first of these seems to be
a more sombre relative of the simple and childlike tunes of the
Presto; at its first appearance it is accompanied by the
persistent rhythm of B from Ex 85 and it can be seen from the
quotation:

Ex 86

that at the end of the first and fifth bars the second violin plays
under it a little phrase strongly reminiscent of the first three
notes of the fugue subject (Ex 52) with which the whole work
begins. This resemblance is emphasised a few bars later
when the tune is transferred to the bass and the three-note

F

phrase is played above it; in all probability the thematic connection is deliberate. As in several other of Beethoven's later works, the second subject, in E major, makes a tantalisingly brief appearance. It consists mainly of a short phrase of great tenderness, repeated several times over very simple tonic-and-dominant harmony, with frequently recurring directions for *poco rit* which make a peculiarly appealing contrast with the relentless rhythmic energy of the movement as a whole. But this brief moment of repose is soon swept away by a long and strenuous development, based entirely on the main theme. At first it is given in its entirety in F♯ minor; then the phrase marked B takes the stage and moves still further in the subdominant direction against a simple but very impressive counter-subject of ascending semibreves. Eventually A returns in B minor and its first three notes are then worked against a running counterpoint. Soon the dominant of C♯ minor is reached, but there is a period of prolonged suspense, very characteristic of Beethoven, ending with a remarkably impressive passage in three-bar rhythm over an increasingly rapid two-note ostinato.

After this elaborate preparation a note-for-note recapitulation of the first theme would have been an anticlimax, and, as in the first movement of Op 59, No 2, the opening bars are extended. B has a new counter-subject reminiscent of the first part of the development and Ex 86 appears in F♯ minor, not accompanied by the rhythm of B as it was at its first appearance. As in the first movements of the Piano Sonata, Op 111 and the Quartet, Op 130, the second subject, kept severely in check in the exposition, is allowed more say in the recapitulation. A passage reminiscent of the later part of the development leads to the very remote key of D major, already used for the second movement, and it is here that the second subject is recapitulated. Then, still more unexpectedly, it is repeated in C♯ major, which at this particular moment sounds not like the tonic major

but like a strange dreamlike region even more remote than D
major. It is obvious that the music cannot stay here for long
and it is soon firmly established in C♯ minor, and ready to
embark on an enormous and very eventful coda. A vigorous
passage built on A is interrupted by the last complete appearance of Ex 86; when it is repeated in the bass the resemblance between the three-note phrase above it and the fugue
subject is made more definite. Soon the two elements of the
main theme return and there is a magnificent climax:

Ex 87

in which B is combined with a simple but very powerful
counter-subject which seems to balance the rising semibreves
that appeared in a similar passage early in the development.
After this tremendously energetic outburst, the rest of the coda
is more changeable in its moods. There is a mysterious passage
which looks back for a moment to D major, a key that has
several times played an important part in the work. After a
short burst of energy there is a beautiful passage based on the
first four notes of Ex 86. The descending sequence with which
it opens recalls a similar passage in the first movement of the
String Trio in C minor from Op 9. The last stages of the movement are concerned with the first three notes of A and the
rhythm of B. There is a series of plagal cadences ending on the
chord of C♯ major, the last three being marked 'poco adagio'.
In the final bars the rhythm of B asserts itself vigorously, but
the feeling of the passage as a whole is sombre and tragic.

When sending Op 131 to the publisher, Beethoven described it as 'odds and ends pilfered from various sources'. Marion Scott made the very interesting suggestion that the Fugue may originally have been connected with the Mass in C♯ minor on which Beethoven is known to have been working at the time. Certainly it would be hard to find any other work of his containing so wide a range of mood. Its plan might well have seemed more unconventional in 1827 than forty or fifty years earlier, when composers were writing divertimenti and similar works in which the order of movements was decidedly variable. The scheme is graded and balanced with great sensitiveness, the Andante, which is the most elaborate and perhaps the most elusive part, being the centre-piece. The key of C♯ minor is reserved for the movements at either end and it is in these and in the short Adagio that precedes the Finale that the most tragic music is to be found. Of the two lighter sections, the quieter and milder, the Allegro molto vivace in D major, is placed after the Fugue, at a moment where a lightening of colour is necessary, but where the more exuberant high spirits of the E major Presto would have been jarring. On the other hand, after the constantly changing moods and atmosphere of the variations of the Andante, the uninhibited hilarity of the Presto is highly effective and the change from it to the deep pathos of the Adagio, quasi un poco Andante, is one of the most powerfully dramatic strokes in the work. It may be that the C♯ minor Quartet contains nothing that makes quite as overwhelming an impact as the Cavatina from Op 130. But taken as a whole, it may be said to be at the same time the more varied and the more closely unified of the two quartets. In both works Beethoven was able to achieve, in the far more intimate medium of the string quartet, the capacity to 'embrace everything' that Mahler regarded as an essential qualification of a symphony.

12

Op 135

THE Quartet in F major, Op 135, has none of this 'all-embrac-ing' quality; it is concise in form, spare in texture and intimate in mood. This reticent quality is particularly noticeable in the first movement; it has more thematic material than any of the other sonata-form movements in the last five quartets, but the ideas are all rigorously controlled and never allowed to expand. The opening at once suggests an atmosphere of quiet and sophisticated conversation; the first phrase:

Ex 88

has a questioning air similar to that of the Piano Sonata in E♭ major, Op 31, No 3, but with a touch of irony. The more flowing melody that follows is divided between various instruments and leads to an oddly enigmatic phrase in octaves:

Ex 89

With all its conciseness the movement refuses to be hurried and has time for yet another theme which leads in a suave and leisurely way to the second group. This is brisk and animated, with lively triplet movement and melodic phrases such as:

Ex 90

that in themselves have a decidedly Haydnesque feeling. But the texture is more contrapuntal than would normally be found in a Haydn exposition and the mysteriously bare colouring of Ex. 91:

Ex 91

could hardly come from anyone but Beethoven in his latest manner. After a codetta of great charm, the exposition ends with a reference to the second half of Ex 88. The development opens with a closely wrought contrapuntal passage built on the first phrase of Ex 88, Ex 89 and an arpeggio in triplets reminiscent of the second group. The second part of Ex 88 then appears and pretends for a moment to return to the tonic. Finally the first note of Ex 88, complete with grace notes, asserts itself persistently against a counterpoint in triplets and eventually expands into a broad statement of the opening phrase, which, for the first time in the movement, appears in a confident mood, without its usual furtiveness. This marks at the same moment the end of the development and the beginning of the recapitulation. The most important new feature of this concerns Ex 89, which appears in a varied version in quavers, decorated with chromatic notes. This, again, is worked contrapuntally against the first phrase of Ex 88, first for a few bars early in the recapitulation and also at greater length in the coda. Here the combination of these two ideas forms the basis of a passage particularly characteristic of Beethoven in its broad alternation of tonic and dominant harmony, which stands out with particular spaciousness against the generally epigrammatic character of the whole movement. It is followed by reminiscences, first of the codetta and then of Ex 88. During the course of this the opening phrase makes its final appearance loudly, in octaves, but it is the latter part of the theme that has the last word, in a quietly informal way eminently suited to this rather elusive but singularly fascinating movement.

The next movement, Vivace, is as energetic as the Presto of the C♯ minor Quartet, but with a decidedly sardonic undercurrent. This is first apparent when, after the very simple and innocent main theme has run its course, a persistently reiterated E♭ has the effect of an extraneous intrusion which has no effect whatever on the general course of the music; there is no eventual explanation, as in the case of the equally unexpected C♯ in the Finale of the eighth symphony. Grotesque in a more obvious way is the return of the main theme with its two outer parts doubled in octaves and contrapuntally inverted:

Ex 92

The fact that, in the words of Dr Fiske, 'for the latter part of this section the music seems to slip back half a century' adds to the general oddness of the whole passage. Equally unusual are the proportions of the movement, the Trio being far longer and more eventful than the main sections. As in the Presto of the C♯ minor Quartet, this begins in the tonic, but it modulates further afield. The succession of keys, F, G and A, is very unusual for the time and while it is taking place a small and seemingly unimportant rhythmic figure of five notes becomes more and more insistent. Then the music is firmly fixed in A, this figure is played fifty-one times by all the instruments except the first violin, who indulges in a wild and angular dance above it. The whole passage has an atmosphere of nightmarish obsession, similar to that produced by Elgar in the third movement of his second symphony. When this has exhausted itself, there is a very unceremonious return from A major to F major and the first part is repeated. There is a short coda which consists entirely of chords in F major in a syncopated rhythm reminiscent of the mysterious E♭'s and ends with a loud and abrupt ejaculation. It is interesting to note that Vaughan Williams, who was not in sympathy with Beethoven's music as a whole, deliberately and consciously 'cribbed' (his own word) two of the most prominent features of this movement for the triumphal dance for Satan in *Job*.

The first two bars of the slow movement move from F to D♭ by the very simple method of slowly building up the chord of the latter, starting from F. The result is comparable in impressiveness with the first bar of the Adagio of the Piano Sonata, Op 106. The movement itself is a set of variations so simple and strict that its form seems to have been unobserved by several writers. The theme itself is only ten bars long and is magnificently planned. The opening phrases move entirely by step, after which the compass is gradually extended by arpeggio-like phrases and culminates in a widely sweeping curve. The dark, rich colouring looks back to the central movement of the 'Appassionata' Sonata and is often associated by Beethoven with the key of D♭ major. In the first variation it is lightened and decorated with chromatic touches of great beauty; the melody remains fairly close in general outline to that of the theme. The second variation, in C♯ minor, is marked 'più lento' and is slightly freer; the second phrase moves temporarily to the relative major, but it is sufficiently close to the theme to be considered a variation and not, as d'Indy would have it, a central episode. It opens in a profoundly sombre mood and its broken phrases and unrelieved block harmony give a strange sense of oppression. In the third, the major key returns and the melody of the theme is played by the cello and imitated in free canon by the first violin. There is also considerable independence in the central parts and the contrapuntal texture is liable to produce some unusual harmonic progressions. Towards the end there is a slight increase of semiquavers in the second violin and viola parts, which prepares the way for the quietly flowing movement in the final variation. In this there is no hint of the melody of the theme, the first violin playing a series of short phrases over a simple but subtly spaced accompaniment. There is some deeply expressive chromatic colour, but the harmonic outline of the theme can be felt, and its deliberate movement, after the more contrapuntal

texture of the previous variation, is so spacious and reposeful that only two bars of coda are necessary in order to
round off the set. One of the most remarkable features of the
last five quartets is the dissimilarity of the four sets of variations
that are to be found in them. The 'Heiliger Dankgesang' from
Op 132, with its alternating Lydian and major tonalities, is
perhaps the most original, and the Andante of Op 131 the most
complex and the most varied in mood and texture. The Adagio
of Op 127 achieves the most perfect balance between the claims
of variety and unity; the slow movement of Op 135, with its
short and sublimely simple theme, is concerned above all with
concentration and continuity. With it Beethoven's long career
as a writer of variations comes to an end, and it would be hard
to imagine a more perfect conclusion, or a truer realisation of
the phrase 'Süßer Ruhegesang oder Friedensgesang', which
Beethoven wrote against one of the sketches.

Far more debatable is the significance of the mysterious
phrases that are prefixed to the Finale: 'Der schwer gefasste
Entschluß' over the whole movement, 'Muß es sein?' over the
theme of the introduction and 'Es muß sein' over the first
theme of the movement itself:

Ex 93

What was the question that caused him so much difficulty and
indecision? Suggestions have included 'Must I die?', 'Must I
go to the trouble of writing another movement?', 'Must I pay
my laundry bill?', 'Must I let you have more money?' (to his
cook). And there is a further possibility that Beethoven,
realising perhaps that one theme was a melodic inversion of the
other, added the words later. There is certainly a sense of

emotional uncertainty, which can be felt in the introduction
when the canonic texture of the opening bars is almost immediately swept aside by gruff ejaculations. The main part of
this Finale has something of the same brittle and elusive
quality as the first movement; its general atmosphere suggests
not a heroic resolution or affirmation, but a kind of half
ironic cheerfulness. The 'Es muß sein' phrase is soon succeeded
by a subsidiary idea which has a strong resemblance to the
second half of the fugue subject from the C♯ minor Quartet.
The second main theme, which appears in the unusual key of
A major, appears to be a gay and artless relative of the melody
of the slow movement:

Ex 94

and is presented against a suitably simple background; 'Es
muß sein' appears at the end of the exposition and, more
emphatically, at the beginning of the development. It is then
worked contrapuntally with the subsidiary theme and gives
place to the second subject, now in block harmony. But soon
the subsidiary returns and leads the music into an atmosphere
far more sombre than anything that we have yet met in the
movement.

This culminates in a powerful return of the introduction;
instead, however, of the opening canonic texture, the 'Muß es
sein?' theme appears under a tremolo. This is remarkable for

its use of the augmented triad, a chord which has since succeeded the diminished seventh as an all too easy means of producing tension, but was far less hackneyed in Beethoven's day. The 'Es muß sein' theme appears in the slow (Grave) tempo, with curiously moving effect. The recapitulation is decidely free, the subsidiary theme, which was so prominent in the development, playing a smaller part here. After the return of the second subject in the tonic, however, there is little change till the coda. At the beginning of this 'Es muß sein' appears with strangely hesitant harmonies:

Ex 95

which seem to belie the words. It is cheerfully brushed aside by the second subject which is given first with all four instruments playing pizzicato and then under lively counterpoint. Finally 'Es muß sein' returns in a more confident mood, first in a whisper and then loudly and defiantly.

It is appropriate to the part played by Beethoven's string quartets in his whole output that they should end, not with a monumental structure on the scale of the ninth symphony but with a short and intimate work like Op 135. In its extreme terseness it recalls the Piano Sonata in F♯ major, Op 78, for which Beethoven himself had a particular affection, and in all probability his last quartet meant at least as much to him as its slightly earlier predecessors. In spite of its small dimensions it contains an astonishing variety of textures. The solemn richness of the slow movement, perhaps the most immediately appealing feature, has parallels in earlier works, but the sudden outburst of tremolo in the Finale was at the time a very new effect and one that has sometimes been overworked by later writers of chamber music. In the other direction, Op 135 shows more predilection than any of the other posthumous quartets for the bare, spare contrapuntal writing, such as is found in the third variation of the Andante of Op 131, or the passage from the first movement of Op 127 quoted in an earlier chapter as Ex 44. Sometimes this linear approach results in surprising harmonic clashes as in the very impressive passage that leads to the dramatic return of the introduction of the Finale:

Ex 96

To underrate so subtle and prophetic a work as this would be grossly unfair; on the other hand it is equally misleading to see it as a kind of summing up of Beethoven's achievement as a quartet writer. The Quartet in C♯ minor, with its spacious and immensely varied structure, seems to come as a crowning climax after the three works that preceded it and it would have been hardly possible for Beethoven to continue in the same direction. Reference has already been made to his love for doing the same thing in different ways and it is highly characteristic of him that he should have followed the three monumental quartets in A minor, B♭ major and C♯ minor with a laconic and in some ways oddly disquieting work. The slow movement of Op 135 has something of the same serenity and profundity as the magnificent Arietta of the Piano Sonata in C minor, Op 111, but, though not necessarily greater, it is certainly terser and more economical. And in the other movements the elusive and sometimes abrupt understatement often seems to look ahead, not so much to the later nineteenth as to certain aspects of the twentieth century. In the still later Finale written eventually for Op 130, Beethoven, despite occasional outbursts of gruffness, seems in the long run to have achieved an almost Haydnesque gaiety and mellowness, though at the same time often looking ahead to later things. But Op 135 is far more enigmatic. The extraordinary outburst at the end of the Trio of the Scherzo has no parallel in any other of his works; in the Finale, whatever views we may have about the seriousness of the words written above two of the themes, we may feel that, although the simple 'Es muß sein' theme appears more frequently and has the last word in the final bars, it is the feverish questioning of 'Muß es sein?' that remains most vividly in our minds.

13

Conclusion

REFERENCE has already been made to certain thematic resemblances between Op 130, 131 and 132, which have led Paul Bekker and other writers to believe that the three works were conceived as a vast triptych. Since then, Deryck Cooke has discovered another basic theme:

Ex 97

which, with fascinating ingenuity, he has traced, not only in these three works, but also in Op 127 and 135. But matters of this kind must be approached with great caution, as is exemplified only too clearly in Rudolph Reti's *The Thematic Process in Composition*. When writing about works of a pre- or post-classical kind, such as Palestrina's 'Iste Confessor' Mass or Debussy's 'La Cathédrale engloutie', he is most convincing. But when dealing with the eighteenth or nineteenth century, he constantly points out resemblances that can only hold water on the very unlikely assumption that the composers of that period thought of their ideas solely in terms of melodic line without any reference to either harmony or rhythm. It is for instance very hard to believe, as Mr Reti would have it, that there was any connection in Beethoven's mind between the first and second movements of the Piano Sonata in C♯ minor; such melodic resemblance as exists between them is completely nullified by other considerations. Even when the resemblances go further than the melodic lines, it is fatally easy to trace them in music written at a time when there were so many stock phrases used by all and sundry. It could be held, for instance, that when Mozart wrote the set of six quartets dedicated to Haydn he deliberately unified them by writing decidedly similar themes for the first movement of the first quartet in G major and the last movement of the last quartet in C major, and that the same idea can be found in the Andante of the Quartet in E♭ major, and, if a sufficient number of notes are omitted, in the Finale of the Quartet in D minor. Furthermore, there is a marked resemblance between the themes of the Minuet of the A major Quartet and the first movement of the C major; possibly the notes of the ascending triad with which the A major Minuet opens could be regarded as an inversion of the descending triad with which the first movement of the Quartet in B♭ major opens. But Mozart himself might have felt some surprise if his own ingenuity had been pointed out to him.

Connections of this kind are less easy but not impossible to find in the music of Beethoven, even though his melodic idiom was less stylised. Among his earlier works the most obvious instance of thematic resemblance is that between the second subjects of the first and last movements of the 'Kreutzer' Sonata, but unfortunately the Finale was originally intended for Op 30, No 1 and was only shifted to the 'Kreutzer' as a last-minute change. It may well be that in his later years Beethoven was increasingly interested in new methods of unification; the thematic connections between the movements of the Piano Sonatas Op 106 and 110 are almost certainly intentional. But, following in Mr Cooke's footsteps, it is possible to see the Piano Sonata in E major, Op 109, as providing thematic links between the other two. The outline of the theme of its first movement shows, in a different way, the preoccupation with rising and falling thirds that is so characteristic of Op 106. In the theme of the Finale the falling third predominates and in both the second and the fifth variations there are moments when the entry of different voices gives the effect of falling thirds alternating with rising fourths which plays so important a part in the first movement and Finale of Op 110. And from this, as Mr Cooke says, it is but a step to the theme quoted as Ex 97. There is a deep fascination in tracing connections of this kind; in the words attributed many years ago to a classical lecturer at Cambridge: 'It may be spoof, but it's spiffing spoof.'

But our whole-hearted acceptance of Mr Cooke's theories must depend in the long run on the extent to which we regard the posthumous quartets as 'a more or less self-enclosed area of Beethoven's output'. He castigates the works of the second period for their 'blatantly optimistic character which the nineteenth century so adored and the twentieth century finds so hard to swallow' and quotes as instances the third, fifth and seventh symphonies and the 'Emperor' Concerto. But surely this is a highly one-sided view that takes no account of the stormy tragedy of the 'Appassionata' Sonata, the mellowness of the Cello Sonata in A major and the Violin Sonata in G major, Op 96, the subtle grace of the Piano Sonata in F♯ major, the gaiety and tenderness of the fourth symphony or the terse abruptness of the F minor Quartet. Mr Cooke stresses, very rightly, the introvert character of the last quartets, but, in varying degrees, this quality can be found in all Beethoven's music, and it has already been suggested that there was particular scope for it in the essentially intimate medium of the string quartet. In the last works his imagination became increasingly subtle and far-reaching, sometimes, as in the slow movement of Op 132, wandering into mysterious and unfamiliar regions and sometimes, as in the 'Grosse Fuge', showing a structural power of unprecedented monumentality. But the exuberant high spirits of such a movement as the Presto in the C♯ minor Quartet are no less extrovert than similar things in the earlier works and, although the idiom has in some ways changed, it may be doubted whether the posthumous quartets contain anything more deeply thoughtful and serene than the Adagio of Op 59, No 2, or more delicately subtle than the Allegretto of Op 95. It is worth recording that Busoni at one stage reacted against Beethoven's middle-period works, especially the third symphony. But his complaint was not that the music sounded too optimistic, but that it suggested a state of permanent bad temper. Perhaps his and Mr Cooke's strictures between them constitute a back-handed compliment.

In view of the infinite variety of Beethoven's works, early, middle and late, it is not surprising that the various sections of his output have made their influence felt in an astonishing diversity of ways. Perhaps the most obvious manifestation of it is the immense breadth and spaciousness of outline which was to culminate in the opening of the ninth symphony and have effect on so much later music; the slow harmonic build-up at the beginning of 'Das Rheingold' and the ruthless harmonic reiterations in the Dance of the Adolescents in 'Le Sacre du printemps' might possibly claim the same ancestry. This side of Beethoven's style can be felt in the string quartets, but less markedly than in the symphonies or piano sonatas; their influence can more often be traced in matters of detail and texture. But so much chamber music was written towards the end of the eighteenth century that it is not always easy to disentangle influences and to decide who did what before whom. A strong influence in Beethoven's early life was that of Aloys Förster, at whose house he heard much music and may also have had lessons in quartet-writing. Several string quartets and quintets by him are published in the 'Denkmäler der Tonkunst in Österreich' and have decidedly Beethoven-like features. The first movement of a Quartet in F minor, published in 1799, has strong affinities with that of Beethoven's C minor

Quartet from Op 18; still more striking is the opening of a
slightly later Quintet in A minor:

Ex 98

and several works in minor keys end quietly in the tonic major,
much as Beethoven had done some years before in the Piano
Trio in C minor from Op 1 and the String Trio in the same key
from Op 9. In a case like this it is impossible to decide on the
priority of inspiration. Förster was many years older than
Beethoven and a glance at the thematic index of his works in
the D.T.Ö. volume suggests that his earlier works were more
leisurely and elegant in style than the later ones. It is probable
that Beethoven's early chamber music was played in his
house and it may be that the older man was influenced by the
dynamic personality of the younger.

Of the composers born during the last years of the eighteenth century the one who felt the most whole-hearted
sympathy for Beethoven's music was undoubtedly Schubert. It
would hardly have been possible for him to have remained
impervious to the influence of the older man, but it would
have been equally impossible for so individual a composer to
be submerged by it. In his early instrumental works there are
more traces of Haydn and Mozart than of Beethoven and, as
Sir Jack Westrup has pointed out, it was their orchestral rather
than their chamber works that affected him most. Of
Beethoven's earlier chamber music, he seems to have been
influenced less by the Op 18 quartets than by the String
Quintet, Op 29; the opening of this foreshadows that of

Schubert's Piano Sonata in B♭ major, and its Finale the Quartet Movement in C minor. In their different ways the slow movements of all three of Op 59 probably affected him, especially the serene leisureliness of the Adagio of the second and the wistful melancholy of the Andante of the third. And the Adagio of the F major Quartet, like the Funeral March of the 'Eroica', could well have inspired some of the startlingly powerful and dramatic outbursts that occur in so many of Schubert's later slow movements. The scherzos of his String Quartet in G and String Quintet in C show the influence of the third movement of Beethoven's Op 74 and the first movement of the D minor String Quartet has Beethoven-like features, including a phrase that comes straight from the first movement of the Cello Sonata in D major, Op 102. But the movement also shows the essential dissimilarity of the two composers' methods. Beethoven would have treated the rhythmic phrase with which the movement opens with greater insistence and would have allowed less latitude to the lyricism of the second subject. Mention has already been made of the resemblance between the opening themes of the finales of Beethoven's Op 130 and Schubert's Piano Sonata in B♭ major, but on the whole the increasingly expansive lyrical flow of Schubert's latest works led to regions far removed from the posthumous quartets, and the suggestions of Beethoven that occasionally appear in them, such as the opening of the Piano Sonata in C minor, show more kinship with the works of the second period.

Berlioz, another fervent admirer of Beethoven, has described a performance of the C♯ minor Quartet given before a decidedly hostile audience in Paris. His own reactions are interesting; at first, his suspicions perhaps aroused by the fugal texture, he feared that he would be bored, but soon he was carried away by the music, in company with a very small minority. In his own wayward and unpredictable melodies there is hardly any suggestion of the influence of Beethoven, but an unusual harmonic progression such as Ex 99:

Ex 99

from the C♯ minor Quartet, has a decidedly Berliozian flavour. It is hard to imagine Berlioz ever taking much interest in the composition of chamber music, yet in his more restrained works, such as 'L'Enfance du Christ', he could achieve a sense of remote serenity that may well owe something to the posthumous quartets.

Mendelssohn felt a life-long devotion to Beethoven's music and was keenly interested in the last quartets at a time when they were generally considered repellently eccentric. The Quartet in F minor, Op 95, was also a particular favourite and in his own A minor Quartet, Op 13, he showed that, though steeped in the influence of this work and, still more, of Beethoven's Op 132, he could write music of considerable power and individuality. In his slow movements a desire to emulate the grandeur of Beethoven was apt to lead to sentimentality, but in this early work this was held in check by the salutary influence of the fugal episode from the Allegretto of Beethoven's Op 95. Many years later, when writing his own Quartet in the same key (Op 80), Mendelssohn again came under the spell of Op 95, but in general the texture of his string-writing was much more akin to that of the 'Rasumovsky' Quartets and Op 74 (especially its slow movement). Often when writing for string quartet Mendelssohn seems to long for the more varied colours of an orchestra, and at no time did he emulate the spare texture so often to be found in Beethoven's last quartets.

Schumann, still more than Mendelssohn, expressed himself naturally in a rich texture, but his more withdrawn and introspective temperament was nearer in spirit to Beethoven's last quartets, of which he made an intensive study before writing his own three. Just as Mendelssohn's contrapuntal skill served as a healthy corrective to his more sentimental side, so in Schumann's music the influence of the square, domestic German student-song was modified by his love for veiled hints and understatements, with mysteriously blurred formal outlines. It is this that gives his music its singular fascination, and although his actual ideas do not often suggest Beethoven, the way in which they are presented, often with the minimum of formality and with wayward and unexpected shifts of emphasis, seems to combine certain features of Beethoven's later style with a domestic tenderness peculiar to Schumann himself. The F minor Quartet, Op 95, left its mark on Schumann as on Mendelssohn; the slow introduction to the Finale must surely have suggested the haunting little piece 'Thema' from the 'Album for the Young'. And the intimate lyricism and thoughtfulness of the first two movements of Beethoven's Op 127 undoubtedly found echoes in Schumann's quartets, especially the slow movement of Op 44, No 2, in F major.

There could be no greater tribute to the profundity and manysidedness of Beethoven's late quartets than the fact that, in very different ways, they have affected the music of three composers as dissimilar in personality as Berlioz, Mendelssohn and Schumann. Of these, Mendelssohn had at the same time the most fluent technique and, on the whole, the most limited imagination; none of them can be said to have had the architectural power of Beethoven. The construction of instrumental works on a large scale played an important part in the output of Brahms; his deep affection for traditional forms led his admirers to hail him as the successor of Beethoven and one or two obvious but unimportant thematic resemblances lent colour to this. In his *Sturm und Drang* moods, especially when writing in either C minor or F minor, Brahms could strike a note of Beethoven-like defiance and one of his finest slow movements, the Adagio of the String Quintet in G major, is decidedly reminiscent, both in theme and in general mood, of the third movement of Beethoven's Op 59, No 1. But, with the possible exception of the Finale of Op 132, it was middle rather than late Beethoven that affected him most and the nostalgic melancholy of his latest works has little in common with the posthumous quartets.

Wagner wrote ecstatically about the C♯ minor Quartet, and here and there can be found passages, such as the 'La Malinconia' section of Op 18, No 6 and the introduction of the first movement of Op 59, No 3, in which Beethoven, in order to create temporarily an atmosphere of mystery, uses a chromatic style which was later to become one of the most important elements in Wagner's mature work. But his debt to Beethoven was concerned less with harmonic detail than with broad outlines, and it has already been suggested that for this the symphonies would have affected him more obviously. In some ways the 'Grosse Fuge', with its enormous dimensions and elaborate thematic transformations, comes nearer to Wagner than anything else in the quartets, and he may have studied it, though it is doubtful whether he would have had much chance of hearing it. For very many years the posthumous quartets continued to be regarded with profound suspicion by a large number of musicians, and it is amusing to learn that Gounod, of all unlikely people, was accused in 1862 by the critic of the *Revue des Deux Mondes* of being a composer who, 'in company with all the bad musicians of modern Germany, be they Liszt, Wagner, Schumann, or even (for certain equivocal things in his style) Mendelssohn, have drunk at the tainted spring of Beethoven's last quartets'. In the latter half of the nineteenth century the increasing pre-occupation with rich colouring inevitably led to a decrease of interest in the string quartet. Dvořák, who wrote more of them than most of his contemporaries, was an eclectic genius who could absorb many influences without losing his individuality; the genial and full-blooded lyricism of his quartets is more akin to Schubert, and occasionally to Haydn, than to Beethoven. At this stage the influence of the late quartets can be felt from time to time, not in matters of general style or texture, but in isolated cases in which an individual theme has made some kind of impact on an individual work by a later composer. The connection between the first movement of Borodin's first string quartet and the Finale of Beethoven's Op 130 has already been mentioned. The introduction to the first movement of Glazunov's String Quartet in A minor must have been influenced by that of Beethoven's Op 132 in the same key. The second subject of the slow movement of Brahms's fourth symphony has a strong affinity to the theme of the Lento from Beethoven's Op 135. The 'Muß es sein?' theme from the same work has found echoes in the sombre motive:

Ex 100

which opens the fourth scene of the second act of 'Die Walküre', and in the openings of Liszt's 'Les Préludes' and of Franck's symphony. In the last of these the alternating tempi im-mediately suggest the opening of Beethoven's Op 130.

But all these resemblances, though interesting, are comparatively superficial; it was at a later period that the spirit of the late quartets began to make itself felt in more far-reaching ways and it is a testimony to their great variety that their influence is felt in strikingly dissimilar ways. It has already been suggested that the slow movement of Op 132 was in many respects the boldest piece of music that Beethoven ever wrote, and it was not till many years later that a composer used a modal tonality, not as an archaism but as a means of exploring new ground. Sibelius, in the central movement of his early Piano Sonata, wrote alternating sections where the contrast is not between modal and major, as with Beethoven, but between slow Dorian and quick Phrygian. The result is attractive, though a little naïve, and probably prepared the way for later and more assured ventures. In the fourth symphony the very flexible tonality is full of modal suggestions, mainly Lydian, and the two outer movements of the sixth and passages in the seventh contain music that has at least something of Beethoven's rapt serenity. Many years later Bartók, in the slow movement of his third piano concerto, wrote a chorale-like theme presented in a manner very similar to the opening of the 'Heiliger Dankgesang'; it has great beauty, but gives the impression that Bartók, at this stage of his career, was not, like Beethoven, calmly contemplating new horizons but looking back wistfully at the past.

During the present century the reaction against the rich texture of the music of the Romantics led to an increasing interest in the aspects of the last quartets which had for many years been found the most forbidding. Even Ernest Walker, in his in many ways admirable monograph on Beethoven written in 1905, regarded the Fugue in the C♯ minor Quartet as a mystery and the 'Grosse Fuge' as quite beyond the pale; both of these are now admired as two of Beethoven's most remarkable achievements. The former was in itself a landmark owing to its remoteness from the energy, sometimes rather

perfunctory, of most contemporary fugal writing. It was
followed, after a considerable interval, by a variety of des-
cendants. Bartók's first quartet, written in 1908, and Hindemith's third, written in 1922, both open with a slow fugal
movement, and in both cases there is a deeply thoughtful
atmosphere not unlike that of Beethoven's C♯ minor fugue.
In both cases this atmosphere is not sustained but gives place
to music of a more declamatory character. Many years later
Hindemith began his fifth quartet with a slow fugal movement
in which the opening mood is continued throughout; less fugal
than this, but possibly nearer to Beethoven in spirit, is the very
sombre slow movement which opens Shostakovich's eighth
quartet and returns at the end, in a more elaborate form. By a
curious coincidence the themes of these two movements:

Ex 101

Ex 102

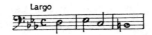

begin with the same succession of notes, D, E♭, C, which has a
decided affinity to the opening of the C♯ minor Quartet (see
Ex 52); but anyone who wishes to attach a mystic significance
to this must bear in mind that Shostakovich's theme had
already been used in the third movement of his tenth symphony
and was intended as a musical representation (D, Es, C, H)
of letters from his own name. It is possible also to find something of the spirit of the 'Grosse Fuge' in the Finale of Shostakovich's seventh quartet, in which the fiercely insistent counterpoint of the first half merges strangely and unexpectedly into
a wistful dance built on a transformation of the fugue subject.

Of the three modern composers whose quartets have just been mentioned, Hindemith is on the whole the furthest removed from Beethoven. With all his solid technique and fine musicianship, his emotional range is limited and his texture, sometimes reminiscent of Reger in its elaborate detail, is apt, when he is not at his best, to descend to a fussiness which is the antithesis of the far more sweeping and varied methods of Beethoven. The development of Bartók's career as a composer of string quartets has decided analogies to that of Beethoven; making allowances for differences of date and idiom, the contrast between Bartók's middle- and late-period works is not unlike that between the 'Rasumovsky' and the post-humous quartets. For the brooding and sometimes bitter introspection of Bartók's sixth quartet and the more genial waywardness of the fifth it is possible to find parallels in Beethoven's last works. But as was pointed out in an earlier chapter, Beethoven in his last works could still be whole-heartedly and sometimes riotously gay, but in Bartók passages of this kind usually have a flavour of irony. We are too near to the quartets of Shostakovich to have an entirely clear view of them; but in the last five at least there are decidedly Beethoven-like qualities. Apart from the influence of individual move-ments, the frequently spare texture, the wayward variations of mood and the willingness to write on occasion the simplest of tunes against the simplest of backgrounds—all these suggest that Shostakovich has learned much from Beethoven's posthumous quartets without the slightest sacrifice of individuality.

It was pointed out in an earlier chapter of this book that a composer's string quartets are bound to show him in an aspect different from that presented by his symphonies. In Shostako-vich's quartets, as in his preludes and fugues for piano, the idiom is more intimate and sensitive than in at least some, though not all, of his symphonies. It is significant that Bartók, certainly one of the great quartet-writers of this century, wrote no symphony, and Hindemith has written decidedly less symphonic than chamber music. But, with the exception of Schubert and Mendelssohn, the great Romantic composers wrote more symphonies than quartets, and the same is true of Haydn and Mozart. One of the most impressive indications of the colossal range of Beethoven's genius is the fact that he, greatest and most widely loved of symphonists, should notwithstanding have written more quartets than symphonies and shown an increasing interest in this branch of composition in his last years. Nothing can be gained by exalting either portion of his work at the expense of the other; Wagner expressed his views in words with which many will agree: 'Give me Beethoven's symphonies and overtures for public performance; his quartets and sonatas for intimate communion.'

General Index

Index to Beethoven's Works